The Skull of Iron Eyes

In a remote forested valley, six miners, led by the once famous magician Will Hayes, strike pay dirt. As it turns out, a fortune in golden nuggets is hidden throughout the length of the dense landscape, waiting to be gathered up and taken back to civilization. A small isolated tribe of natives are the miners' only obstacle but Hayes has a dastardly plan. . . .

All goes well for Hayes and his ruthless followers until they make the mistake of killing a child and casting her body into the river. What none of the miners realize is that the body will be found by the infamous bounty hunter Iron Eyes. He vows to discover who killed the little girl and he won't stop until he sees justice done. . . .

The Skull of Iron Eyes

Rory Black

A Black Horse Western

ROBERT HALE · LONDON

© Rory Black 2010
First published in Great Britain 2011

ISBN 978-0-7090-9081-6

Robert Hale Limited
Clerkenwell House
Clerkenwell Green
London EC1R 0HT

www.halebooks.com

Typeset by
Derek Doyle & Associates, Shaw Heath
Printed and bound in Great Britain by
CPI Antony Rowe, Chippenham and Eastbourne

Dedicated with love to my eldest daughter Lucy Jane.

PROLOGUE

San Remo was never the quietest of towns yet it was about to get a whole lot noisier as darkness fell. The sixty or so buildings which encircled the courthouse and spiralled out in a half dozen different directions began to glow as their lamps and lanterns slowly erupted into light. The sound of tinny pianos and guitars flowed from the saloons and cantinas as the strange sight of a man dressed in undertaker's clothing and steering his tall palomino stallion into the very centre of the busy settlement overwhelmed the onlookers.

Few sights could have chilled their souls quite as much as that which greeted them in the flickering amber illumination. The eyes of those who saw the bounty hunter atop his tall mount would never see anything as frightening again. For this was no ordinary rider who had arrived in the midst of the southern Texan town. This was a man who was here for one reason and that reason was to kill.

Iron Eyes stared with cold calculating eyes all around him at the street whilst he sat motionless astride his powerful mount and allowed it free rein. His boots were dug deep into his stirrups and his reins were looped around his saddle horn. The bounty hunter sat with both hands on the grips of his Navy Colts which poked out from his pants belt. Iron Eyes was ready for anything that might occur. He missed nothing as the horse walked on down toward the large whitewashed courthouse.

People gasped at the sight of the stranger in San Remo. Even though none of them had ever seen the bounty hunter previously they all recognized death when it rode into their town.

Iron Eyes reached forward, tugged back on his reins and stopped the stallion right outside the tall white building. His long right leg looped over the horse's mane of golden hair and the thin emaciated man slid down to the ground. The sound of his razor-sharp spurs rang out as though warning of the danger which now loomed over anyone who got on the wrong side of the bounty hunter. He paused beside his saddle and glared over the shoulder of his tall horse at those who seemed to be frozen to the ground at the very sight of him.

People began to run as he tied his reins to the nearest hitching rail. They ran as though the Devil himself had entered San Remo's boundaries.

His eyes darted up and down the boardwalk before he stepped up on to it. He had seen the many various saloons as he had entered the large town but had kept on riding.

There was only one reason for which he had now stopped his search for his elusive prey, and that reason was directly across the street. The five lathered-up mounts outside the Golden Bell saloon bore testament to the fact that they had only recently stopped fleeing the man who was walking towards them.

Iron Eyes raised both arms and ran his thin fingers through his mane of long black hair. He then heard more gasps from those who saw the brutalized face he now revealed.

Without missing a step the bounty hunter jumped down from the boardwalk and continued across the street at pace towards the saloon. The sound of music rang out over the swing doors. Yet Iron Eyes did not hear anything. His entire concentration was now focused on only one thing: locating the Barton gang and killing them.

They were worth $2,000 in total.

He pushed his way between the five exhausted horses. They all began to shy and vainly fight their restraints. He had the aroma of death upon him and even weary horses could smell that loathsome scent.

Iron Eyes stepped up outside the saloon and then rested for a few moments. He looked hard at the horses, then nodded to himself. They belonged to Ben Barton and his four cronies, he thought. He turned and took two steps. He paused and glared over the swing doors until satisfied that the men he sought were somewhere within this building's four walls.

Even choking tobacco smoke mixed with the unmistakable smell of stale liquor could not hide their putrid odour from his flared nostrils. He knew his prey well.

They were in there OK.

Just as he was about to enter the smoke-filled saloon he heard a man clearing his throat beside him. The bounty hunter stopped. His head tilted slightly as he looked through the limp strands of hair at the man who was less than five feet from him. Iron Eyes would have ignored most men who dared to stop him when he was ready to go after his chosen goals but this man wore a tin star on his vest.

'What you want, Sheriff?' Iron Eyes asked in a low mumble.

The sheriff felt his heart quicken when he saw the hideous scars on the face of the tall thin figure. He swallowed hard and took another step toward the bounty hunter. 'Who are you?'

'They call me Iron Eyes,' came the swift reply.

'What's your business in San Remo?' the lawman pressed.

'I'm here to kill five varmints,' Iron Eyes answered.

'I'm a bounty hunter and they're all wanted, dead or alive.'

Joe Hawkins was a man who would never see forty again. For a quarter of his life he had been elected sheriff for San Remo and its surrounding county. Yet in all his days he had never once felt as scared as he did looking at the tall man dressed more like an undertaker than a bounty hunter.

'W . . . who?' Hawkins croaked.

'Ben Barton and his boys.' Iron Eyes took his eyes off the sheriff and returned his attention to the people inside the Golden Bell. 'You seen them?'

Hawkins shook his head. 'Nope. Never even heard of them.'

The thin left hand of the bounty hunter rested on the top of the swing doors. 'Now's your chance.'

The lawman went to speak but it was too late. He watched as the bounty hunter energetically pushed the doors apart and marched into the busy saloon. Hawkins trailed the man with the long flowing hair who pushed others aside as he forged on towards the back wall of the drinking hole.

'Barton!' Iron Eyes screamed out loudly.

Wanted outlaw Ben Barton was sitting with his two brothers Lee and Kit at a poker table. They had already accumulated three near-naked females and an equal amount of whiskey bottles. Now in horror they saw the man whom they had wrongly believed they had managed to shake off their tails days earlier.

'Iron Eyes,' Ben Barton snarled.

'Go for them guns.' The bounty hunter stopped and kicked the closest table between them away. 'Draw!'

They did. As the females screamed out the trio of outlaws dragged their guns from their holsters and started to fan their hammers. Yet Iron Eyes had matched their speed and pulled both his Navy Colts from his belt. As bullets exploded into action the thin man pulled back the hammers of both his weapons and squeezed their triggers over and over again. Iron Eyes felt the heat of their lead as it ripped through the tails of his long black coat. But his expression did not alter as he stood firm. He had seen his own lead tear open their chests in quick succession. Blood spewed over the yelping women as they tried to scramble away from the bleeding bodies which had them pinned down behind the poker table.

Hawkins caught up with the bounty hunter and stared at the men as they slid from their chairs on to the sawdust-covered saloon floor. Pools of crimson spread out as the bar-room girls fled in hysterics to the bar. 'You killed them.'

Iron Eyes did not respond. He turned and looked around the saloon. Each face with its open mouth was studied in a mere beat of his heart until he was satisfied.

'What you looking for?' the sheriff asked.

'The others,' Iron Eyes snarled.

'What others?'

'Whip Slater and Clem Barker,' the bounty hunter replied. He strode across the floor of the saloon until he cornered one of the still sobbing girls. He pushed one of his guns into his belt and grabbed her arm. He pulled her towards him. The blood of the Bartons still covered her exposed breasts and dripped from her nipples on to her blue satin dress. 'Answer me.'

Her eyes widened as they locked on to his mutilated features. 'Who are you? Why'd ya do that?'

He shook her arm and silenced her. 'Where's the other two varmints them critters rode into town with? They upstairs with some of your friends? Where are they?'

'I don't know,' she screamed out.

Then a deafening shot rang out across the saloon. Iron Eyes released his grip, spun on his heels and stared to where he could see both Barker and Slater as they headed towards the swing doors. A score of men and women stood between the bounty hunter and the outlaws. Gripping one of his Navy Colts in his right hand, Iron Eyes took a step. Both men fired their guns again.

The bounty hunter stopped. He was confused. They had not shot at him but up at the ceiling. Then he heard a sound. Iron Eyes looked up and saw the wooden chandelier falling. Its securing rope had been severed by one of their bullets.

13

Iron Eyes went to move but it was too late.

The full weight of the chandelier crashed down on to him. He felt his head splitting open as he hit the floor. He could see the candles burning in the sawdust just before he heard the sound of the two outlaws' horses as they thundered away.

The thin man tried to rise but he could not.

Then everything went black. His mind became a whirlpool and he felt himself falling into a place he knew only too well.

ONE

The forest flourished in the heat that radiated off the surrounding land. Heat rose through the jungle-like density of the brush, creating clouds of steam and moisture. An eerie mist hung like phantoms throughout the forty miles of valley, unable to escape the steep sides of the mountains. Vines were intertwined with trees of every kind making it virtually impossible for all but the most determined and skilful of souls to pick a path between them. The deep floor of the valley had a fast-flowing river coursing along its entire length, whilst to each side tree-covered mountains stretched heavenward and loomed ominously over everything below them.

This was a place where few from the outside world had ever ventured. Yet those who had dared to risk their lives in the almost impenetrable forest had quickly realized the opportunities that this mysterious place offered those willing to take full advantage of its innocent inhabitants.

The band of six prospectors led by the seasoned Will Hayes had never turned down a bonanza and they certainly were not going to start now. Hayes had once been an accomplished illusionist and magician in San Francisco, when the first gold nugget had been discovered. Since that fateful day he had spent his every waking moment dreaming of discovering the mother lode.

Each day, leading their horses and packmules, the six hardened goldminers had ventured deeper and deeper along the valley. The further north they went the more signs they found of the abundant wealth the forest held for anyone willing to claim it. After the first few days of their exploration they had accumulated more gold nuggets than it was possible to carry.

The miners carefully buried their finds for when they returned south but none of them, including Hayes himself, had any idea of what additional treasures awaited them further up the river.

They were soon to find out. For several nights they had seen the red glowing light of a giant campfire dance across the waters of the river. It lit up the forest right up to the very top of the mountainside. It drew the curious men like moths to a flame.

Set deep in the densest part of the forest a mere ten miles from the end of the valley, a structure made of wood and mud had stood for so long that none of the natives who lived near by knew anything about it. To them all memory of who had built it had gone. For centuries it had simply stood apart from the much smaller similarly constructed structures in which the natives lived. Each night the Indians built a new fire so large that it was guaranteed to keep all beasts away.

All four-legged beasts, that was. None of the Indians knew that they were being spied upon by a far more dangerous animal from the shadows.

Totems dotted throughout the valley seemed to tell a story of flying gods in their carvings, and that had intrigued Hayes. The showman sensed, in his soul, an opportunity. He had once made a fortune using his skill as a magician to fleece those who had either faith or superstition. The sight of the Indians bestowing gifts at the entrance to the big building told him that there was something here that he could exploit.

Hayes correctly suspected that the large domed building might still be filled with the gifts placed within it by the Indians' long dead forebears. For rituals are hard to shake; even when the reasons for those rituals have been forgotten they tend to continue on.

As Hayes and his men had looked on they had no idea that their wildest dreams were actually true. Golden trinkets encrusted with precious jewels filled the large edifice, although the centuries had virtually covered them from view. No longer remembering how to manufacture the precious ore into works of art the natives now simply placed crude gold nuggets at the building's entrance.

Will Hayes and his cohorts had found the small village and its innocent inhabitants. They could see the golden rocks gleam as the light of the giant campfire illuminated them. To the miners this was their only god.

The only thing they worshipped.

Like so many of their breed who dreamed of finding El Dorado they knew that this place was probably the closest any of them would ever get to achieving that elusive goal.

Hayes knew that they could simply have entered the village and killed the natives to get their hands on the gold, but that would be to kill those who, he knew, might be turned into his slaves and deliver more and more of the precious ore to his feet.

Then a plan had started to ferment in his fertile mind. It hailed back to his days as one of San Francisco's finest and most successful magicians.

All it would take was magic and he was a past master at making even the most intelligent of audiences believe anything he wanted them to believe. These were simple Indians who had probably never even seen a white man before. Never known there was another world beyond their tranquil forested valley. They were like children.

Their minds would be like putty in his hands. Will Hayes knew he could control them by using his skill as an illusionist. All it would take was the right trick, and they would be deceived by the most unbelievable of illusions.

A few days later it all fell into place.

Will Hayes had been quick to read the ancient images carved on the now rotting totems. One image stood out for Hayes and that was an image of what appeared to be a flying man. A man who was also a bird. It seemed to be on every totem pole.

A man bird.

For the first time since he had amazed San Francisco's finest with his ability to make men or women float above audiences and even lions seemingly vanish into thin air, Will Hayes knew there was a way to use his unparalleled skills to get what he wanted, to obtain all the gold he desired. Unlike in his earlier days, this time his captive audience would make him and his cohorts rich and believe them to be gods.

Hayes had found his bonanza at last.

The following morning as the six men huddled in the dense brush, hidden from the Indians as they paddled back to their camp in canoes, the oldest and most wily of the prospectors gripped the arm of his nearest companion. Hayes gave out a grunt of satisfaction as the realization of how he could fool the natives suffused his weathered features.

'I've figured it, Bob! I got me the trick that'll fool the whole bunch of 'em!' Hayes exclaimed triumphantly.

The robust figure of Bob Tobey stared hard at his pal. 'Keep ya voice down, Will. Them Injuns might be the type that take scalps.'

'I don't fear no half naked critters!' Hayes laughed.

Tobey was soaked with his own sweat. He exhaled heavily and rubbed his face with large calloused hands. 'Ya mean ya figured out what trick will fool them?'

'Damn right I have!' Hayes sounded different to their ears. He looked as though he was drunk as the idea filled his mind and brought back memories from half a lifetime earlier. 'The trick I once fooled an entire city with. Damn! I was famous back then before I got me the gold fever. This was my biggest trick. It fooled even royalty.'

Pete Brown eased closer. 'I ain't sure about this idea of us going into that Indian camp, Will. You might have a mighty good trick but they might have a lot of real sharp arrows.'

'Them totem poles, boys,' Hayes ranted at the others who huddled close as they watched the strange natives paddling away with their canoes full of fish. 'Ain't you read the pictures on them damn totems? The answer's there.'

Pete Brown leaned over the others. 'What you

mean? How can you read a dumb totem?'

Hayes jumped to his feet and started to lead them from their hiding place out on to the soft muddy shoreline. 'C'mon.'

Like obedient hounds they followed.

Before the Indians had turned up, Sly Rowe, Rance Bean and Clint Henson had nearly broken their youthful backs collecting the unimaginable hoard of gold nuggets which were littered everywhere on both sides of the river. Rowe rubbed the sweat from his face with the palms of his hands and sighed heavily.

'Them carvings ya mean? Is that what's got ya all fired up, Will?'

Rance Bean shook his head and looked at Henson over his shoulder. 'He's gone loco, Clint. It's this damn heat. He ain't never cracked up like this before.'

Henson nodded. 'I ain't sure he was ever a magic man at all.'

'Them's just pictures, Will.' Tobey said bluntly as he watched the Indians disappear round the bend in the river, going to where smoke could be seen billowing from hidden campfires. 'We ought to just go and shoot them savages. Then we can help ourselves to all them nuggets they done collected.'

The men walked to where one of the totems stood close to the river's edge. Hayes stopped, turned to his five comrades and gestured at the carvings on the wooden pole.

'Look at these carvings. Look at the ones where the man turns into a bird. See them?'

'Just native garbage.' Brown dismissed the images.

Hayes took one of his guns from its holster and stared at it. He then looked into the faces of his five henchmen. 'We got us a powerful amount of guns but we don't need them. Them Indians only got themselves bows and arrows and that's just fine. Whatever happens, we get the better of them. I'll have them thinking that we're gods, boys. They'll be eating out of our hands by the time I'm finished messing with their minds.'

'Ya seem awful sure about this idea of a trick fooling them Injuns,' Bean said. 'I reckon the guns are our best bet.'

'The guns are our insurance.' Hayes nodded.

Tobey stared hard at the carvings Hayes had mentioned and then looked at the oldest of their small band. 'A man who turns into a bird? But that ain't possible.'

'What if you seen it with your own eyes, Bob?' Hayes smiled and looked at all their faces in turn. 'What if you all saw a man flying like a bird? What would you think?'

They were all silent.

Hayes rammed his gun back into its holster. 'Before the gold rush back in 'forty-nine I was the best damn magician in Frisco. I've fooled the smartest of folks in my time. I made people float in

22

the air. Made them fly around the theatre over the top hats of some of the richest dudes you ever seen. Made them really think what I wanted them to think. Hell, I can rig up an illusion to fool even the cleverest of people and get them to believe that it was real.'

'Can ya really do that, Will?' Tobey asked.

'That and a whole lot more, Bob.' Hayes reached into his pocket and to their utter surprise pulled out a small trinket that none of the others had seen before. It was a small, well-moulded golden model of a deer. 'See this? I found it a few hours back when you was filling sacks with nuggets. This was made by them Indians or maybe their ancestors. There might be more to be had. Nuggets are good but what if we can lay our hands on a whole load of stuff like this? This is worth a fortune. The nuggets gotta be smelted down. This kinda thing has already bin smelted.'

Bean tilted his hat back off his face. 'You figuring on trying to hoodwink them Indians and getting them to hand over all their golden baubles, Will? With a trick?'

Hayes nodded hard. 'Yep. We gotta make them think that their gods have returned and then force them to hand over all their gold. Let them do all the hard work for us.'

'That's a mighty dangerous thing to attempt, Will,' Rowe observed. 'We ain't got no clue as to how many of them there are up the river. Could be hundreds. That's a lot of folks to fool and keep under control.'

Will Hayes stood. 'I've fooled thousands in my time. Besides we got us guns if they get ornery.'

The sight of the trinket in Hayes' hand made the others realize that there could just be an even greater fortune to be plundered.

'A flying man?' Bean pondered the thought. 'Is that even possible, Will?'

'Yep.' Hayes surveyed the forested slopes which surrounded them on both sides. The mist hung in dense patches along the length of the valley. Hayes pointed in turn to two trees, one either side of the river, then glanced back at his men. 'We have to rig up a line from there to there,' he said aiming a finger at two stout branches. 'The mist will help us a whole lot as well.'

'Why rig up a line across the river, Will?' Bean queried.

Hayes turned to Bean and the others. He showed them the golden deer trinket again. The morning sunlight danced across its beautiful shape as it lay on the upturned palm of his left hand. Hayes mumbled strange words and then passed his right hand over the gleaming model.

It disappeared.

The men gasped.

'Why rig up a line?' Hayes repeated the question. 'How else am I gonna fly over them Indians, Rance?'

TWO

It was a sickening vision which chilled even the most hardened of witnesses to the bone. The sight and the smell of a burning man spread out beneath the broken chandelier amid the dozen candles upon the sawdust-littered floor had stunned them all. Yet only a few moments earlier the bounty hunter had been anything but helpless. His pair of matched Navy Colts lay to either side of his bony hands. Smoke was still trailing from their barrels like snakes seeking more prey. Each of the men and women in the saloon had moved closer as it became obvious that for the moment the deadly Iron Eyes had been knocked clean out by the heavy light fitting which had smashed down on to his unsuspecting skull.

But it was the bodies of the Barton brothers which stopped even the most drunken of them from venturing too close. The bullets which had ended Ben Barton and his brothers' lives had proved that the strange thin figure was a cut above anyone else who had ever visited San Remo.

Even unconscious and alight, Iron Eyes had the ability to frighten people. They kept their distance not through respect but from sheer fear. Only one man had the courage to close the distance between himself and the bounty hunter. That man was Joe Hawkins.

The sheriff emptied a bucket of water over the smouldering figure on the floor of the Golden Bell. The smell of the bounty hunter's burning hair and coat faded as the water washed the candles across the sawdust-covered boards. A pool of blood from the brutal gash across the top of his scalp had encircled the head of Iron Eyes. A mixture of wooden splinters and candle wax made the injury appear even more horrific.

For a moment the figure dressed in undertaker's clothing did not move. Then his thin bony hands began to twitch. Every eye in the saloon watched as the bony fingers clawed at the boards. Then Iron Eyes coughed and pushed himself up.

'You OK, Iron Eyes?' Hawkins asked nervously. He cast the bucket aside and rested his hand on the grip of his holstered Colt.

The bounty hunter managed to get on to his knees before the pain inside his skull stopped him for a few moments. Iron Eyes coughed again, then continued to push himself off the sodden floorboards. People backed off until nearly everyone in the saloon was pressed against the building's walls.

'My head!' the bounty hunter grunted as he tried to remember what had happened.

Hawkins leaned over but kept a respectful distance between himself and the hands of the deadly bounty hunter. 'Yep! You got a mighty bad chunk of scalp ripped up there.'

Iron Eyes rolled over until he was seated. He blinked hard and touched his bleeding scalp. Droplets of blood trailed along the strands of his hair before dripping on to his lap. It did not trouble him, though. He had endured far worse. Iron Eyes looked at the gore on his fingertips and then at the man with the star on his vest. 'Did someone hit me?'

'Nope,' Hawkins replied, pointing at the three dead men on the floor behind him. 'You killed them varmints and then a couple of others shot the rope holding up the light fitting. It fell on to your head.'

Iron Eyes sighed and scrambled like a newborn fawn to his feet. He swayed for a few seconds, then managed to straighten up to his full height. With blood covering his features he looked even more hideous than before.

'What's that smell, Sheriff?' he asked, his nostrils flaring.

'That'll be your hair,' the lawman answered. 'Them candles set fire to that mane of yours. Lucky I put it out before you ended up like me.'

27

'What?' Iron Eyes kept a hand on his head and focused on the sheriff as Hawkins removed his Stetson briefly to reveal his bald head. 'Oh.'

Hawkins moved to the towering figure and then bent down and picked up the two Navy Colts. He was surprised at how light they were in comparison to his own .45. He handed them to the bounty hunter who poked them into his belt. 'Ain't you got a gunbelt, boy?'

'Never liked them,' Iron Eyes said as he felt his blood dripping through his fingers.

Hawkins looked towards the Barton brothers again. 'You sure they're wanted dead or alive?'

'Yep.'

'I ain't never seen no circulars on them critters,' the sheriff said drily. 'I don't imagine you can prove they're wanted dead or alive, can you?'

The bounty hunter lowered his bloody hand and rammed it into one of the pockets of his tail coat. He pulled out a few crumpled Wanted posters and pushed them into Hawkins's hand. 'That good enough?'

Hawkins studied the posters and gave a nod. 'Yep. That'll do just fine. I'd have hated if you had turned out to be some loco killer who just roamed around shooting folks for no reason.'

'I never kill folks for no reason, Sheriff.'

'I'll take your word for that.'

Iron Eyes blinked hard. He still could not see

straight and it troubled him. 'You happen to see which way the other two members of the gang went, Sheriff?'

'I sure did.' Hawkins smiled.

The bounty hunter's ice-cold stare fixed upon the tier short lawman. 'You gonna tell me?'

'In good time.'

'What?' Iron Eyes gritted his teeth. They were small and sharp, like an animal's.

'First I'm gonna take you to get that head of yours sewed up.' Hawkins grabbed the emaciated figure's bony arm and led him through the crowd. They did not stop walking until they reached the boardwalk. The fresh air hit them both but it was Iron Eyes who seemed to dislike it most. As the swing doors of the saloon rocked on their hinges the bounty hunter swayed and staggered. Only the wooden porch upright prevented him from falling face first into the street. Iron Eyes clung to the upright as he sucked in air and vainly attempted to make his eyes work properly.

'You OK, Iron Eyes?' There was genuine concern in Hawkins's voice as he wrapped an arm around the injured man.

'My eyes!' The bounty hunter gasped. 'I can't see straight. Every damn thing is blurred.'

'I figured as much.' Hawkins pulled the man, who seemed to weigh far less than his size would suggest, away from the porch support. 'I'll take you to the doc's.'

'All I need is whiskey.' Iron Eyes closed his eyes. His head felt as though a thousand Apache warriors were beating their war drums inside his skull.

'You and me both, boy.' Hawkins helped the man down the street towards the wooden sign with the simple word 'Doctor' painted upon it.

As they walked Iron Eyes dragged a cigar from his pocket, rammed it into his mouth, then found a match. His thumbnail struck the match into flame and he sucked in the smoke deep and long.

'You kill a lot of folks, Iron Eyes?' Hawkins asked.

As smoke drifted from his mouth the thin man answered, 'A few, old-timer. A few.'

THREE

No Fourth of July could have equalled the show which the once famed magician created that night six months earlier in the depths of the forest. Using the skill honed like a straight razor decades earlier William Hayes had brought the remnants of a once mighty tribe to their knees in less than ten minutes flat. It had been a concoction of fire and water masterfully orchestrated to bend even the strongest of minds into submission. It had been a work of genius, considering that Hayes had only what was carried on their packmules' backs to work with. Wire, ropes, black powder and sheer guts had been enough, though. Enough to fool the unsuspecting eyes of the innocent natives.

Hayes had learned his trade well. Even after endless years of chasing his dream of striking it rich by finding gold where others had failed to do so, he had lost none of his mastery when it came to the art of illusion.

As he had always said, it was all in the presentation. Even a poor trick could appear good if you had enough flames and swirling smoke surrounding it. This trick was good, however, and the addition of smoke and flames simply added to its overall effect. Hayes and his five cohorts had rigged up a series of wires and ropes across the width of the river during the day. Then the master of illusion had carefully used the contents of one barrel of gunpowder to make a dozen crude Roman candles. He knew how to control the deadly black powder so that it obeyed his commands. Black powder only exploded if confined in an outer casing when ignited. Placed either in a loose tube or even on the ground it would flare but never explode. A thousand magic tricks had proved that fact.

Smoke and mirrors.

Hayes had no mirrors but the reflections off the river were an acceptable substitute for a man with imagination. The smoke was easily created and mixed with the valley's natural low-hanging mist.

The unsuspecting Indians had been peacefully preparing for the coming of another night around their campfire when Hayes had started his show. The stunned and terrified natives had witnessed the five heavily disguised figures moving towards them along the river's edge. Each of the miners was throwing fireworks ahead of him. The carefully controlled explosions and smoke terrified an already frightened people into virtual submission before Hayes had even finished his prologue and made his own well-crafted appearance.

The five miners had been covered in mud and leaves to such an extent that it was virtually impossible to see any human outline in their forms. As the tribe cowered before the big domed building, filled with precious offerings, Bob Tobey gave out a guttural roar and held a smoking stick of black powder heavenward. As it spat out venomous curled fire it blended with the eerie moonlight, mist and smoke. Then, dressed as some strange birdlike creature, Hayes leapt fearlessly from the branches of a tree on the opposite bank with two blazing torches in the hands of his outstretched arms.

He flew majestically across the river with the grace of a man half his age. The fast-flowing water below him reflected the flames of his torches and frightened the Indians even more. Fiery smoke trailed him until he reached the place and he knew would be the key to his illusion's finale. Hayes discarded his torches ahead of his men. The five miners threw handfuls of black powder at the torches and a cloud of acrid smoke shielded Hayes from view for a brief moment. He disappeared behind the branches of a tree less than twenty strides from his wide-eyed audience.

It was enough time for him to release himself from the hastily constructed harness and drop to the ground. A horrific birdlike mask and swooping wings made from branches and leaves suddenly became something far more frightening in the eyes of the people who watched him march out in front of his five followers, pluck the blazing torches up again in his hands and wave them at the natives.

A scream went around them. They were so stunned that none of them had even thought of picking up their weapons. All they could do was to look at what had presented itself.

Then more explosions followed as Rowe and Henson threw their explosives into the river. Plumes of water sprayed over the camp as the six men made their victorious unopposed entrance.

From that moment the half-dozen miners had become gods just as Hayes had predicted. From that moment on they ruled the innocent people who had seen a man bird fly into their lives.

The prospectors forced the naïve Indians to bring them more and more of the valuable golden rocks which were scattered throughout the forested valley. Their appetite was insatiable.

Hayes and the others could simply have gathered up what was already inside the big building and become far wealthier than they might ever have expected in their wildest imaginings, but that would have been too easy.

For these men had suddenly become gods.

They were worshipped and feared. They had their pick of the females and knew that their firepower could crush any objections the Indian braves might raise. They had enslaved an entire tribe.

It is not easy to turn your back upon being a god.

Smoke and mirrors.

Yet sometimes even the wisest of men can be fooled by their own elaborate illusions. Sometimes smoke can blind not just the audience but also the performers.

It was a dazed Iron Eyes who reluctantly entered the doctor's office accompanied by the sheriff and stared through the long limp strands of blood-soaked hair at the old man seated before a cluttered desk. He was still unsteady on his long thin legs and he swayed beside the lawman. The doctor rose, made his way to the two men and studied them in turn. It was obvious who required his expertise.

'What we got here, Joe?'

'This is Iron Eyes, Doc.'

'Sit down, Iron Eyes,' Doc Lowe said in a gruff voice which did not suit his fragile frame. 'Let me get a good look at that head of yours.'

The unsteady bounty hunter did as he was told. He sat upon the hardback chair beside the desk and glared at the man who peeled the hair away from the brutal gash across the top of his torn scalp. Iron Eyes felt the fingers probing the wound as the doctor bent over and looked straight at him.

'That skull of yours don't feel right, boy.'

'What you mean, Doc?' Hawkins asked.

'Feels like a busted egg shell,' Lowe answered severely.

The sheriff rubbed his chin. 'That don't sound good.'

'It ain't,' Lowe retorted. 'How'd this happen, Joe?' The doctor went to the corner where an enamel bowl was sat beside his stove.

Hawkins watched as Lowe poured some hot water from a kettle into the bowl. He knew the entire story was too gruesome to recall in detail. 'The chandelier in the Golden Bell fell on this poor critter's head.'

The old doctor made a tutting noise as he returned to his desk and placed the bowl on top of a pile of papers. He opened a drawer and pulled out a roll of bandages.

'How'd you feel?' Lowe asked the bounty hunter.

'I've felt better,' Iron Eyes growled back.

Doc Lowe cleaned the wound. He continued to tut. 'Any ill effects?'

Iron Eyes sighed. 'I can't see straight.'

'A few days rest will see you OK,' the doctor ventured. 'Leastways, I hope it will. That skull of yours feels as though its been cracked apart, though.'

Hawkins pulled out a pipe from his vest and placed the stem between his teeth. 'You could get a room over at the hotel, Iron Eyes. They got real fine beds in there. I don't reckon you ought to be riding for a while.'

The bounty hunter sighed. 'I got me vermin to catch and kill.'

Lowe bent over and squinted hard at the wound. He carefully picked out splinters of wood embedded in the torn, bleeding scalp. 'This sure is a mess. Reckon I'll have to pour some surgical spirit over this before it gets infected. Then I'll sew it up.'

'Ain't you got no whiskey?' Iron Eyes asked. 'I'm powerful thirsty.'

Lowe pointed at the closed bottom drawer of his desk. 'I got me a bottle of whiskey in there but—'

The doctor did not have time to finish his sentence before the bounty hunter's long thin left arm dragged open the drawer and retrieved the bottle of amber liquor. He pulled its cork with his teeth and spat it across the office before downing a long swallow. He then handed the bottle to Lowe.

Lowe looked at Hawkins and shrugged. 'I reckon I could put it on his bill.'

Suddenly without warning, Iron Eyes lowered his head and gave out a groan. He then stood and screwed up his eyes as if in agony. Both men watched as the bounty hunter grabbed both sides of his head. He staggered across the office and bumped into the far wall.

'What's wrong, boy?' the sheriff asked, rushing to

the tall, swaying figure's side.

The doctor moved cautiously to the other side of the bounty hunter and held the man's nearer arm. 'Easy, son. Don't panic. What's wrong?'

Slowly Iron Eyes lowered his hands from his head. He turned and faced both men. Blood continued to drip from the limp hair which covered most of his face. He opened his eyes and blinked several times. Even his scars could not conceal the fear etched into his face.

'What's the matter, Iron Eyes?' the sheriff pressed. 'Tell Doc what's wrong.'

Lowe held his grip on the bounty hunter's arm. 'Tell me, son. I'm sure I can help you.'

Iron Eyes swallowed hard.

'I can't see nothing. I'm blind.'

FOUR

The girth of the heavily built man made most others stand aside when he approached. It was as if he had a barrel hidden under his large coat. A bullet belt crossed his chest in which a variety of different calibre shells were neatly held in dozens of hand-tooled pockets. It told even the most guileless person that this was a man who lived by the gun. Many guns. Yet it was the pristine Remington Frontier .44 hanging across his pants studs in a crude but effective holster which caught the eye before anything else. Its black metal finish and wooden grip looked well used. The notches carved into the grip supported the theory.

Kansas Drew McGinty was a powerful man by any standards. Built more like a bear than a man he walked with swaying powerful shoulders along the dark street from the direction of the livery stables. The smell of freshly discharged gun lead hung along the boardwalk outside the Golden Bell as the huge outlaw approached the saloon. Yet for McGinty the scent of freshly fired weaponry was so familiar that he hardly ever noticed it any more. The only thing on the big man's mind was finding a bottle of whiskey and a willing female.

The light of the saloon cascaded out into the dark street. McGinty rubbed a sleeve across his bearded face and licked his lips as he rested a hand on the top of the swing doors. Then his black eyes narrowed as they looked into the oddly quiet drinking hole.

He inhaled deeply. Then he knew that there was another kind of smoke lingering inside the Golden Bell, besides the regular cigar and pipe variety.

Gunsmoke.

The big man could see the still shaking and weeping girls huddled together at the corner of the bar counter. For a breed that tended to use every opportunity in which to trap their next client, the females seemed totally distracted. He drooled at the sight of the bare breasts hanging like ripe fruit over the tops of their dresses. McGinty rubbed his groin and then saw that one of the bar girls was feverishly trying to wipe something off her flesh.

Excitedly, the outlaw pushed the doors inward. He walked slowly towards the women with only one thing on his mind. It had been a long ride to San Remo and there was only so much bouncing up and down on a hard saddle a man could take before something inside him awoke. Something which he had never been able to ignore.

Then, as he got within ten feet of the females he heard men talking across the saloon. He paused, rested a hand on the grip of his gun and turned.

'That Iron Eyes critter sure was fast,' one man said.

'I seen faster,' another drunkenly argued.

McGinty seemed to grow a few inches as he absorbed the name of the bounty hunter. It was a name he knew well. He was about to approach the men when he saw the blood. A lot of blood.

It was splattered up the far wall. The burly outlaw hesitated when he saw what lay crumpled on the floor. The three bodies with the bullet holes in them looked expressionless. The Barton boys were well-known to McGinty. He had ridden with them three times over the previous two years. Each time he had profited by the collaboration. McGinty rubbed his beard and gritted his teeth angrily. They were the only reason he had ridden to this remote town. Ben Barton had promised him the biggest payday of his entire life.

Now that promise lay congealing.

The brothers were lying shoulder to shoulder in an ocean of their own red gore. The bullet holes in them were all dead centre, just as he knew Iron Eyes liked to place them.

A fire started to burn inside him. It was the fire that he had wrongly thought was extinguished. He

41

swung away from the hideous sight, marched to the bar and rested both his hands upon its wet counter.

'What'll it be, stranger?' the bartender asked in a tone which defied the fact that there were three dead men lying less than spitting distance away.

'Whiskey,' McGinty answered in a low growl.

'Bottle?' the bartender asked as his left hand hovered over an array of bottles set behind him.

'Bottle,' the outlaw confirmed. He thumbed a coin from his coat pocket and slammed it down.

'Bottle it is. You sure missed one hell of a play in here a while back,' the bartender said, exchanging the bottle for the coin. 'Never seen such shooting.'

McGinty lifted the bottle, tore its cork from the glass neck and spat it away. 'Iron Eyes?'

The man behind the bar raised his eyebrows. 'Why yes. That was his name. Funny-looking critter. Long hair like an Apache but he was no Indian. Killed them boys with hardly a waste of bullets. Never seen such shooting. Heard he was a bounty hunter and them boys were wanted. Still, it ain't a good way to go.'

The outlaw filled a glass and downed the whiskey. 'This Iron Eyes varmint, was he a tall and thin critter?'

'That's the man.' The barkeep nodded vigorously. 'Ugly as sin itself.'

'Iron Eyes.' McGinty mumbled the name and repeated the action of filling and emptying his glass three more times. Hard liquor filled him with fumes but it was nothing compared to the non-alcoholic fumes that were brewing up inside the outlaw. 'Where'd he go?'

The barkeep polished a glass thoughtfully. 'I think he was carried out of here by the sheriff. Yes. That's what happened. I reckon the sheriff was taking him to see the doc.'

McGinty looked hard at the man with an apron wrapped around his middle. 'Why'd the sheriff take him to see the Doc? Was Iron Eyes wounded? Did one of the Barton boys manage to shoot him before he done for them?'

The barkeep stepped closer to the counter and leaned over.

'A couple of other varmints started shooting at that bounty hunter and brought the damn chandelier down on top of that thin critter's head. With him knocked senseless they high-tailed it and rode out of town. I sure don't blame them none.'

McGinty glanced across the room and saw the wooden wreckage of the chandelier. His eyes returned to the bartender. 'I reckon he was hurt bad.'

'Just stunned. That kind are too mean to die like respectable folks,' the barkeep said. He placed the gleaming glass down next to a score of identical glass vessels.

'Damn it all!' McGinty snarled, pounding his left

43

fist down on the bar counter. Glasses fell from where they had been stacked and were hurriedly rounded up by the bartender. 'I ain't seen Iron Eyes for more years than I can recall and yet he's still blessed by the Devil himself. No real man deserves that sort of luck. Ain't he ever gonna die?'

'I take it he ain't a friend of yours?'

'I got me a score to settle with him, friend,' the outlaw answered fast and hard. 'Only his blood will settle it. You hear me, barkeep? Only him being dead will pay the bill he owes me.'

'What he do?' the bartender tactfully enquired.

'He killed my brother,' McGinty replied loudly. 'Just up and killed him.'

'Why'd he do that?'

McGinty shrugged. 'For the reward.'

The bartender backed away. 'Oh.'

The outlaw tilted his head. He looked to where the females were still chattering like a flock of frightened hens. His eyes surveyed each and every one of them. He had never been in a saloon where the bargirls displayed their wares so openly before. He looked at each of their sets of breasts like a man choosing a chicken for the pot. He drooled and ran a hand down his wild beard before sliding his bottle across the damp counter towards them. He followed it until he was looming over them.

One of the women was still frantically rubbing a spittle-laden handkerchief over her pink flesh. He leaned over and studied her chest, then raised his eyes to her face. Her make-up was smeared down her cheeks but it made no difference to the outlaw. He had already seen her ample bosom.

'What you looking at?' she asked.

'What you trying to rub off there, little lady?' McGinty asked. 'Them nipples are stuck on, ya know.'

Edna Hart was at least thirty and had long lost the first bloom of youth, but in towns like San Remo it did not matter. As long as a female was willing to raise her petticoats high enough and spread her legs, she could always earn a living.

'I'm trying to get this blood off me,' Edna replied in a jerky tone.

McGinty's eyes lowered again. He could see no blood. 'I figure you done a mighty fine job.'

The other girls moved around the burly stranger like flies around an outhouse. They were buzzing at the prospect of a new man to fleece.

Edna did not like the competition. She pushed close up to the outlaw, placed a long red fingernail on his chin, the grabbed hold of his beard. 'I can still see drops of blood. It come off them boys me and the girls were favourin' when that scarecrow shot them. I was drenched in the damn stuff. Can't you see it?'

McGinty felt his head being pulled down until his cracked lips were brushing her skin. He inhaled hard. The scent of stale sweat and cheap body powder filled his eager nostrils. He liked it.

'See 'em?' Edna asked, fending off the other bar-girls with her free arm. 'See the blood?'

'Yeah. I see 'em,' McGinty lied as his tongue rolled out from his mouth and licked her flesh. 'I can taste 'em as well.' Edna gave out a girlish giggle.

One of the other girls named Maisy reached round the narrow gap between the outlaw and Edna. Her small hand pushed the holstered Remington aside, then she pulled at the pants studs until they gave.

McGinty's eyes flashed to his side. He saw the smiling female who had already slid her hand into his pants. He smiled.

Maisy gave out a gratified yelp. She had found more than she had anticipated. 'You ain't gonna believe what this boy has in his pants, Edna.'

Edna tossed her head back. 'Big?'

'Big enough to satisfy all of us.' Maisy nodded as she produced the massive sidewinder from its hiding place. 'Look, girls. You could make a walking-stick out of this thing.'

'You like that?' The outlaw sighed heavily.

'What's not to like?' Edna answered. Her eyes widened at the sight of what was in Maisy's small hand.

Kansas Drew McGinty felt himself being led towards the staircase. With all the girls hanging on to various parts of his body he willingly began to ascend the steps.

'What about that Iron Eyes critter?' the bartender called to the outlaw. 'I thought you was all fired up about him?' McGinty reached the top of the staircase and looked down at the man in the apron. He gave out a booming laugh. 'Don't go fretting about Iron Eyes, little man. I'll kill him later.'

The bartender swallowed hard as the bar girls led the burly figure into the nearest room. He turned to a few of his other patrons and shook his head. 'He seems to have gotten over his grief for the moment.'

FIVE

The thin emaciated figure of Iron Eyes had not moved from the spot for nearly an hour. He stood like a statue, staring with eyes that were unable to see anything. Only his expression altered as he vainly attempted to work out why his world had been plunged into darkness. The smell of freshly brewed coffee filled the office as steam issued from the blackened pot. The two older men sat at the desk sharing the bottle of whiskey and watching the bounty hunter with a mixture of fear and sympathy. Yet even though Iron Eyes claimed to be unable to see, their attention was on the pair of deadly Navy Colts which ominously jutted from his belt above his flat belly.

The well-worn gun grips looked as though they might be drawn into action at any given moment. Doc Lowe picked up a towel, stood and moved across the room to the coffee pot. Gingerly poured three cups of the strong beverage into mugs.

'I reckon that some of my special coffee might help you, Iron Eyes,' Lowe suggested. 'Might get them nerves in your eyes working again.'

Iron Eyes lowered his head. 'Ain't ya got nothing better than stinking coffee?'

'Don't you like coffee, boy?' Lowe asked. The thin tall man refused to move from the spot where he had realized that his eyes no longer functioned.

'Nope,' the bounty hunter drawled.

Hawkins and Lowe glanced at one another, as though they both silently feared that the brooding stranger might decide to take out his fury upon them.

'Gotta agree with the boy, Doc.' The sheriff smiled. 'Some folks can make coffee taste just like trough water.'

Lowe placed all three steaming mugs on his desk.

Hawkins cleared his throat. The scarred head upon the long thin neck turned towards him.

'Doc will fix you up,' he assured Iron Eyes. 'He'll have them eyes of yours working again in no time. No time at all.'

A pool of blood encircled the boots of the bounty hunters who had still not allowed the doctor to sew up his bleeding scalp. Iron Eyes raised his hand and ran his bony fingers over his gaunt face. He gave out a long sigh and carefully turned his entire body until it faced the pair of onlookers.

'Yep! I reckon so. Trouble is I ain't got no time to

waste. I got me two more outlaws to catch and kill.'

'Stop thinking about killing,' Lowe insisted. 'We have to make sure that you're fixed up before you can do anything. That skull of yours needs mending, otherwise it'll kill you just as sure as any outlaw's bullet. Savvy?'

Iron Eyes had his face turned towards where he heard the stern voice of the doctor. There was no visible reaction to any of the words of warning.

'Come sit down here, son.' Hawkins rose to his feet and walked the short distance to the side of the injured man. He guided Iron Eyes to the chair he had just vacated and eased the man down. Iron Eyes had been hurt many times. He had lost more blood in his time than most battlefields had seen wasted upon them but he had always been able to see. For the first time in his entire life he was bemused. His bullet-coloured eyes searched the room, yet they still saw nothing but blackness.

'What you intending to do, Doc?' the bounty hunter asked.

'I'll have to try and put all the pieces of that skull of yours in the right place and then figure out a way of keeping them there,' Lowe answered.

'Cement,' Iron Eyes suggested.

Doc Lowe was about to laugh when he suddenly realized that the bounty hunter might be right. Cement could do the job but he was not sure how. 'Damn it all. Now I gotta be a damn builder.'

Sheriff Hawkins rubbed his neck. 'Could cement be used on a head, Doc?'

The older man nodded thoughtfully. 'Sure enough. If I carefully wrap tight bandages around his skull and then we wet them up I reckon that a sprinkling of cement dust rubbed in could set and hold his skull together. If I did it right, that is.'

'Here, drink this, boy.' Lowe carefully pushed a mug of hot coffee into the bounty hunter's hands. He glanced at Hawkins and shrugged. Both men watched as Iron Eyes lifted the mug to his scarred lips and swallowed the strong black brew in one go.

'How long would it take for my head bones to heal?' Iron Eyes asked.

'I ain't sure.' Lowe leaned forward and filled his patient's mug again. 'I've never had to fix a broken skull before. Most folks with your kind of injury are dead before I gets to see them.'

Iron Eyes gave a wry smile. 'A few days? A week?'

'I don't know,' Doc Lowe admitted.

'Why am I blind, Doc?' the bounty hunter asked forcefully. 'Nothing hit me in the face. Nothing hurt my eyes. I got my skull stoved in and that don't figure. Why can't I see?'

Sheriff Hawkins rested both hands on the bounty hunter's shoulders. He felt the rage inside the seated man. It was like holding on to a coiled spring.

'Easy, boy. Doc will help you. You gotta let him do his work, though.'

51

Iron Eyes downed the coffee, then tilted his head back and looked up at the ceiling. He still could not see anything. 'You said my skull was shattered, Doc. Could that have done this to my eyes? Could it?'

Lowe patted the hands of the bounty hunter. 'I think so. I ain't never had me a patient suffer from this myself but I've read about such cases. We have to fix your skull and then maybe your sight will return.'

Iron Eyes pulled his hands away. He fumbled, then put the empty mug on the desk. 'Do ya worst, Doc. I don't care none any more.'

Lowe looked at Hawkins. 'I reckon you could go down to the hardware store and borrow a cup of cement for me, Joe.'

The sheriff nodded. 'No problem. I'll go when I've drunk that cup of black poison you made.'

Iron Eyes did not understand what was going on but knew one thing for sure. He was now vulnerable. Without his sight he could not see his enemies. He rested an elbow on the desk.

He mustered up his courage and asked the question which was fermenting inside him.

'Could this be permanent, Doc?'

Fearfully Lowe looked at the face of the lawman standing behind the deadly bounty hunter. Hawkins shook his head as if telling him to be careful of his reply.

'I . . . I don't think so.'

Iron Eyes smiled. 'Ya voice got kinda shaky there, Doc.'

'Let's look at this carefully, boy,' Lowe said drily. 'You could see and then suddenly you went blind. Nothing hit you in the eyes so there ain't no actual damage to them.'

Iron Eyes nodded. 'Yeah.'

'I reckon that it must be the fact that you had your head beat up.' The doctor was thinking fast. 'Must be nerve damage. Nothing more than that. If we can fix that skull of yours your sight has to return.'

Iron Eyes tilted his head. 'Enough gabbing. Get started and fix this busted head of mine, Doc. I ain't never liked the dark, to be honest.'

'It ain't that simple,' Lowe explained. 'I'll have to be careful to make sure all the parts of that head of yours is put back right. One false move and I might kill you.'

'Don't fret. I don't die that easy, Doc,' the bounty hunter insisted.

Lowe cleared his throat again and rose to his feet. 'Right! Yeah, I'll start by sewing up the flesh and then I'll have to do the tricky stuff.'

Hawkins walked over to where the doctor had gone. A large glass-windowed cabinet filled with medical instruments faced both men. The lawman watched as Lowe opened the door and started to fill a kidney bowl with all he thought he might need.

'You still want me to go rustle up some cement?'

Lowe nodded. He continued to fill the enamel dish with all the things he imagined he might require.

The sheriff leaned close to the doctor's right ear and whispered, 'You sure you can fix his broken skull, Doc?'

Lowe looked straight into the face of the lawman. 'I have to fix it, Joe. I have to get it right.'

Sheriff Hawkins took a deep breath. 'Right. I'll head on off to Smith's hardware store and borrow a cup of cement. Damned if I'll be able to make old man Smith believe why I only want a cup of the damn stuff, though.'

Suddenly a sound came from out in the street. It was the raised voice of a well-oiled man shouting straight at Doc Lowe's office windows.

'I knows ya in there, Iron Eyes,' the angry voice bellowed out. 'Come on out, ya back-shooting bastard! I'm gonna teach ya it don't pay to kill folks for money. It don't pay to kill my kinfolk.'

Hawkins and Lowe both turned away from the cabinet. To their surprise the bounty hunter was standing and facing in the direction of the shouting man.

'I know that loudmouth,' Iron Eyes growled.

The sheriff rushed across the office to his side. 'Sit down, boy. Doc's gotta fix you up.'

'That's Kansas Drew McGinty,' Iron Eyes mumbled. 'I'd know his pathetic whine anywhere.'

54

'You coming out, Iron Eyes?' McGinty yelled out again. 'C'mon out. I've had me some whiskey and some mighty fine women and I'm ready to kill.'

'I'll go run him off.' Hawkins said to the bounty hunter. 'You stay here.'

Iron Eyes grabbed the sheriff's arm and pulled him back. His grip was like a vice. Hawkins looked up into the face of the bounty hunter and felt his heart quicken its pace. He had never before seen a look like the one carved into the face of Iron Eyes. Even with unseeing eyes the tall man looked exactly the same as he had done when Hawkins had first encountered him outside the Golden Bell hours earlier.

'This is my call, Sheriff.'

'Can you see?' the sheriff wondered aloud. 'Has your sight come back?'

'Nope. I can't see nothing at all.' Iron Eyes released his grip and walked towards the shouting voice. His bony hands located the door and its handle and he opened it wide. He took one step, then lowered his head and continued to absorb the screaming profanities which rained at him. The toe of his left mule-eared boot could feel the edge of the boardwalk just beyond the office door boundary.

Lowe and the sheriff looked at one another. Neither could believe the sight of the defiant tall figure standing in the partly open doorway.

'Ya ready to die, Kansas Drew?' Iron Eyes growled,

flexing his bony fingers at his side. 'Ready to meet that brother of yours?'

McGinty shot out a long sturdy arm and pointed at the man with the light at his back. 'Ain't ya scared, Iron Eyes? Ya oughta be mighty scared.'

'Of what?' came the defiant reply.

'Now I'm gonna finish ya.' Kansas Drew went for his Remington. The sound of the large hand slapping the leather of the holster as the .44 was drawn from its holster filled the quiet street. The bounty hunter raised his arms, pulled both his guns out of his belt in one swift action and blasted out into the dimness. A scream spewed from the bearded man.

McGinty spun on his heels and then, like a felled tree, landed hard on the sandy street. A cloud of dust rose all around his burly figure but Iron Eyes did not see it.

Hawkins went to stand beside Iron Eyes where he stood with the smoking guns in his hands, and gasped at the sight of the blinded man's lethal handiwork.

'Ya killed him.'

'Good.'

'Why'd he come looking for you?'

'He was wanted,' Iron Eyes said. He pushed his guns back into their place in his pants belt. He turned and carefully retraced his steps back towards the desk.

'But why not just ride out? Why face a bounty

hunter?' Hawkins followed the tall man back into the office and closed the door. He saw the expression on Lowe's face. It mirrored his own.

Iron Eyes found the chair and carefully sat down again.

'I killed his brother a year or so back. Reckon he thought he'd get even.'

Doc Lowe waved his left hand in front of the bullet-coloured eyes again. They showed no reaction.

'You're still blind!'

'I know,' Iron Eyes agreed.

'Then how did you manage to hit that McGinty critter with them guns of yours?' Hawkins pressed. 'That *hombre*'s lying out there with two bullets in the middle of his chest. How'd you do that?'

'I could smell him.' The bounty hunter sighed. 'Them McGintys' got a real stink about them. I just aimed where the smell was ripest.'

'You might have gotten yourself killed there, boy,' the sheriff said. 'A blind man taking on a ruthless outlaw is darn dangerous.'

'I told ya, I don't die easy,' Iron Eyes said and sighed.

Joe Hawkins straightened up.

'I'll go get that cement, Doc.'

SIX

The ancient mountains could not tell of the horrific degradation the native people living within its shadows had been subjected to over the previous months. The trees were still green and the river continued to flow along the floor of the valley but the Indians were no longer the same. Their spirits and souls had been destroyed by what they had thought were gods. Having no knowledge or experience of the outside world or its evil ways they had been putty in the hands of Will Hayes and his cohorts. How were they to know anything of what so many of their fellow Indians had been subjected to over the years since their once peaceful land had been discovered? Whether it had been the golden ore which they themselves thought valueless or just the land itself, the result had been the same throughout the vast continent.

How many tribes had simply vanished when the

white men had arrived? Those who had not simply disappeared into the pages of history had been moved from one place to another, from one hell to an even worse one. The Eastern seaboard had once flourished with tribes who farmed crops. Now only their tribal names remained. So many states with names which had once been the proud descriptions of living breathing people were all there was left.

So many had gone. Their only crime was to be living on land others had wanted more. Greed had shown no mercy to the innocent.

The valley now fell silent. The singing had ceased. There was no joy left in the hearts of the broken people who had been deceived into thinking their gods had returned. In six months nearly a third of them had died. Most had fallen victim to the guns Hayes and his followers had brought with them. Some had perished from unseen illnesses against which they had no immunity that the prospectors had carried into the valley. A few had just lost all hope and destroyed themselves.

The eyes of the tribal elder Hakatan burned across the clearing at the large wigwam where the miners had secreted themselves. He had already lost everything he cherished and he wondered when his time would come to join his ancestors. His blood boiled when he saw the miners pick females to abuse each night. Their whips and guns had silenced his and all his remaining braves' attempts to fight back.

Hakatan sat cross-legged inside his small hut nursing his wounds. His eyes never left the large structure occupied by the false gods. At first the females screamed out when the miners had dragged them into their lair. Then they simply accepted their fate, fearing that more of the dwindling number of braves might be either tortured or killed.

Hakatan vainly tried to see an end to their torment.

Unknown to the remaining natives, being regarded as gods had begun to weigh heavily on the shoulders of Will Hayes and his men. There was only so much depravity a man could enjoy before even that became a burden. Now some of them began to wonder how they would ever leave this once idyllic place with the spoils of their ruthless handiwork.

They had taken shelter in the large wigwam as soon as they had triumphantly entered the small village. It had not taken long before they had discovered that the floor of the round building was littered with thousands of precious golden artefacts laid down over untold generations. The miners had bagged them all. Golden nuggets had also been piled up until they reached the height of five feet from the earthen floor.

Each day Hayes had commanded the natives to bring them more and more nuggets as well as food. Each day the Indians had obeyed. Month after month the six men had repeated the actions of the previous one, until they could barely believe how much treasure they had accumulated.

Then it had dawned on them.

How were they going to turn their spoils into hard cash? Even with their horses and mules heavily laden it would take a dozen or more trips back to civilization. Hayes had no magic trick to solve that problem and they all knew it.

The flames of the huge bonfire the natives had lit illuminated the village clearing. Its dancing light allowed the miners to see the hollow hateful eyes of their slaves watching them. So many eyes silently watched them.

It was now the one hundred and eighty third night since they had made the natives believe that a man could fly. It was Sly Rowe who spoke first. His words seemed to say what all the others were thinking.

'How we gonna get all this gold out of the valley, boys?'

Hayes removed his mask and placed it down beside him. He nodded as the words milled inside his mind. 'To get all this stuff out of here we'll have to make us ten or more trips in and out of the valley.'

'Yeah, we just ain't got enough pack animals,' Bean agreed.

The others looked on.

'You mean leave and then come back?' Tobey did not seem to favour the notion. 'Once I get out of this valley I ain't ever coming back.'

'That goes for me as well,' Brown said.

Henson stood and walked around inside of the building. He looked at the mountain of ore and precious golden goods. He paused at the sight of how much they had and knew that each day it increased. His eyes darted to where Hayes sat.

'We could pick a couple of us to take some of this on to Providence whilst the rest of us stays here to keep these Indians under control.'

'Good idea, Clint.' Hayes nodded.

'Hold on a minute,' Bean interrupted. 'What's to stop the ones that goes off to Providence just stealing our share? They might not come back. Without the horses and mules we'd be stranded in this valley.'

Will Hayes smiled and looked at Bean. 'You don't trust ya fellow gold-diggers, Rance? Is that what you'd do? Just keep the gold and forget about the rest of us?'

'Hell! One trip would make them rich.' Bean nodded hard as he waved a finger at the oldest of their group. 'Why would anyone in their right mind return to this valley? It stinks and boils a man's flesh. I figure whoever we chose to leave would never come back here.'

Hayes got to his feet. He moved close to the entrance of the large wigwam and stared out at the other smaller huts dotted beyond the well-fed fire. 'That Indian chief troubles me, boys. I have me a feeling he's planning something.'

Sly Rowe walked to stand beside Hayes. 'Yeah, he's a real troublemaker. We done whipped the skin off his back more times than I can recall and he still don't quit his antics.'

Henson rubbed his hands together. 'Maybe we could all go and take as much gold as we can up to Providence, boys. Cash it up and share it out. Then whichever of us wants to come back here for more can do so.'

'That might work,' Hayes agreed.

'I don't cotton the chances of any of us ever getting back into this camp once we've left,' Brown said. 'We've tricked them and controlled them for months now but once we leave they'll surely not be dumb enough to let us just ride back in.'

Tobey stretched his arms until they clicked and walked to stand beside Hayes and Rowe. 'I'm gonna go down there and get me a female for the night.'

Hayes shook his head. He could still see Hakatan watching them with burning eyes.

'Reckon you better not go alone, Bob,' the older man warned.

'Why not?' Tobey asked.

'I got me a gut feeling about that old Indian,' Hayes replied. He rested a hand on the crude wall of the hut. 'He's planning something.'

Tobey plucked one of their Winchesters up off the ground and cranked its mechanism until the rifle was cocked for action. 'I ain't feared of them. Let any of those fools try anything and I'll put a hole through him!'

Hayes looked at Tobey. 'Just be careful, Bob. If any of us gets hurt or killed them Indians will know for sure that we ain't the gods they think we are.'

Tobey smiled. 'I figure they already know we ain't real gods, Will.'

'Why confirm it?' Hayes sat down and clapped his hands together. 'The longer we can keep them thinking what we want them to think the safer we'll all be.'

Henson walked to Tobey and drew his Colt from his concealed holster. 'I'll come watch ya back, Bob. I could do with a little girl myself.'

As the two miners left the wigwam on their hunt for a pair of females Hayes looked around at the others. 'I sure am glad my sap don't rise any more.'

Pete Brown looked at the man who had masterminded their total dominance of an entire tribe. 'What's ya plan, Will? We staying or are we heading on out? I'll do whatever you reckon is our best bet.'

'I reckon we'll all leave here in the next couple of days with as much of this treasure as our animals can carry. We'll head on up to Providence and get it exchanged for hard cash.'

'You figuring on coming back?' Brown pressed.

'Yep. Only a fool would turn his back on this much loot.' Hayes sighed. 'Once the cash is divided up between us and we get it banked I'm gonna get a score of sturdy mules and come back here with whoever wants to join me. I reckon we ought to be able to get most of this gold out then.'

The men around Hayes did not argue.

They had confidence that their leader had worked everything out and that whatever he chose to do would be the correct course for them to take. His leadership had so far never failed them. Yet none of them, not even Hayes himself, could have known that the magician's earlier concern about the brooding Indian chief was justified.

Hakatan was indeed planning something. Something which went against everything in his nature. For he was a man who had been pushed beyond breaking point. Even though the leader of the small tribe had been taught that mere mortals could never better supernatural beings, he was willing to try.

Things had gone too far.

Hakatan had lost too many of his precious people. He no longer believed that the six strange creatures who continued to torture them mercilessly were worthy gods.

It was a confident Will Hayes who had said that they would leave the valley in a matter of days. The blazing eyes of the Indian chief who feverishly watched two of their strange breed taking a pair of his youngest females back towards the treasure house again had other plans.

Hakatan would try something that his people considered impossible.

He had started to plan how to kill their gods.

SEVEN

Lightning splintered across the vast expanse of heavens above the two riders as they feverishly whipped their exhausted mounts through a narrow twisting canyon. Dust curled up into the night air as the horsemen pushed their lathered-up mounts on and on, as though the Devil himself was chasing them. Both the wanted outlaws knew that they had already achieved the impossible. They had encountered Iron Eyes and were somehow still alive. Smooth, rounded boulders loomed above them, lit by the moon and the fading illumination of thousands of stars which were slowly giving way to the approaching storm. A storm which had dogged their trail ever since they had fled from the distant town.

Both horsemen knew that so far the strange figure who had so expertly cut down their fellow gang members hours earlier had not yet followed. Both prayed that the wooden chandelier had killed him, but they knew that men like Iron Eyes were not easily killed. Glancing back gave neither of the outlaws any feeling of safety or security. Ben Barton had said days earlier that they had managed to shake off the infamous bounty hunter. He had been proved wrong.

Both Whip Slater and Clem Barker knew that just because they could not see the ghostly horseman behind them it did not mean that he was not there.

For men like Iron Eyes never quit. They simply did not know how to stop their deadly pursuit once they had started after their chosen prey. The wanted posters buried deep in the pockets of the bounty hunter had to be honoured. Iron Eyes would never rest until he had caught up with them and sent them to their Maker.

Their horses were slowing. No amount of spurring could get them to increase their pace. At last the cost of the effort expended in the frantic galloping was showing in the way the animals no longer ate up the ground beneath their hoofs but staggered and tripped. It had been a long hard ride from San Remo but neither of the outlaws had noticed. All they could think of was the sight of Iron Eyes when he had slaughtered their comrades in the saloon a few hours before.

It was a vision that had kept both men spurring until they reached the very edge of the moonlit river. The storm was heading their way and neither of them knew whether that was a good or bad thing.

Would the storm protect them or make it easier for the hunter of men to close in on them unseen? It was a fearful question that neither outlaw could answer.

It was Slater who slowed his stumbling mount first. Barker drew rein when he saw his pal ease the lathered gelding beneath him to a halt.

Both men allowed their horses to walk to the lapping edge of the river before they dismounted. As their horses drank Slater and Barker looked back into the strange eerie moonlight at the distant town far behind them. Now sheets of rain were lashing across the barren landscape as the rumbling sky flashed with lethal venom. The storm was getting closer to them and with it came the fear that death would soon follow.

'Ya reckon he's still coming, Clem?' Slater fearfully asked his companion.

'Can't see the bastard,' Barker answered. His gloved left hand held his reins whilst his right rested on his holstered six-shooter.

'That don't mean he ain't still doggin' our trail.' Slater sounded anxious. 'We thought we'd shaken him off days back but he still showed up when we was just starting to have us a good time. Damned if I know how he caught up with us so fast.'

Barker watched his horse drink, then he looked up the steep hillside ahead of them to where a screen of mighty trees stood. He was nervous. This was a land where he had never ridden before. He had tagged along with the Barton brothers and Slater to meet up with a character known as Kansas Drew McGinty. He was just another hired gun.

'I don't like the look of them trees,' Barker said.

Slater gave the forested mountains a brief glance before turning again and studying the trail behind them. The storm was coming after them, just as they feared the strange bounty hunter would do. Lightning forked down in the distance. Both men and horses could smell it. It was like the scent of burning flesh.

'We could ride to the east but that'll add a week or more to our journey.' Slater nodded doubtfully.

Barker screwed up his eyes and kept a firm grip on his reins. 'Where we headed, Whip?'

'Providence,' came the swift reply.

'I ain't heard of the place,' Barker said shrugging.

'It's a gold town,' Slater told him. 'Ain't too many of them left in these parts any longer. Used to be dozens of the damn things scattered all over but they all dried up when the gold started to get hard to find.'

Barker inhaled long and hard. 'Was that critter back there the one they call Iron Eyes, Whip?'

Slater's eyes darted to his companion. 'Did ya get a good look at him, Clem?'

The outlaw nodded. 'Yep. I seen him OK. I ain't never seen nothing that looked like he done. And dressed in the clothes of an undertaker. Face all

70

twisted and curled like something a branding-iron might do if'n it got close to a man's face. I seen him OK. I ain't ever gonna forget that critter.'

'That was Iron Eyes,' Slater spat. 'I heard of how he looks from other outlaws. Never dreamed that them stories could be true but no two men could look that bad. That was Iron Eyes.'

'And he's after us.' Barker swallowed hard.

Slater ran a hand down the chest of his horse. He knew the animal was spent and needed grub and rest. Two items that both he and his partner were a tad short of. 'We'll have to head up into them mountains.'

'Why?'

'Cover and grub,' Slater replied. 'That forest must have plenty of game and I'm hungry. It'll also have plenty of grass for the horses. We can use them trees to cover our backs. Ain't no place to hide out here. Once that scarecrow comes on after us we'll need all the cover we can get.'

Clem Barker shook his head. 'Will we be able to reach Providence by cutting on up through there?'

Slater nodded again. 'I reckon so. We'll follow this river through the forest and if I'm right it'll lead us straight to that gold-mining town.'

'Then what?'

'There's a railhead there.' Slater smiled and gathered up his reins in both hands. 'We'll sell the horses and saddles and buy us a couple of tickets out of this

71

damn country. I reckon we could get to Waco.'

Barker bit his lip. 'Will Iron Eyes quit hunting us then, Whip?'

Whip Slater stepped into a stirrup and eased himself up on top of his tired mount. 'Maybe.'

Barker hauled his own aching frame back on to his saddle and looked back at the storm once more. 'How come I feel like I'm already dead meat, Whip?'

Slater spurred. 'C'mon!'

Both riders steered their horses into the river and towards the forest.

EIGHT

Joe Hawkins had barely reached Doc Lowe's office when the storm unleashed its fury upon San Remo. He led the tall sturdy palomino up into the side alley next to the weathered old building and secured its reins to the porch upright. Then every nerve in his body tautened when a deafening thunderclap erupted directly over the town. The sheriff untied the saddle-bags and was about to step up on to the boardwalk when the rain came. It felt to the old shoulders of the lawman as though he had been caught in a dam-burst. Within a mere heartbeat he was soaked to his long underwear. By the time he had reached the office door and turned its handle he looked as though he had just crawled out of a river.

'Damn it all,' Hawkins protested.

The eyes of the doctor looked up at the bedrag-gled Hawkins as he closed the door behind him and removed his Stetson. Lowe smiled as the sheriff hung his limp hat on the stand next to the window. Hawkins sniffed and glanced at the doctor and his seated patient.

'Ya get them?' Iron Eyes asked.

'Yep. I got them,' Hawkins answered. He walked to the bounty hunter and carefully placed the saddle-bags in the outstretched bony hands. 'Here. I got me soaked as well.'

'Is my horse OK?' Iron Eyes asked as he hung the twin satchels across his lap and patted them.

'He's OK. A tad spooked by the thunder and all but I tied him up firm to the side post.' Hawkins moved to the coffee pot on top of the stove. He filled a mug and then took a sip of the hot black beverage. 'Mighty fine animal that. Never seen a real pure-bred palomino before. Where'd ya get it?'

'South of the border,' Iron Eyes muttered as the doctor carefully patted the last of the cement dust on to the damp bandages which were firmly wrapped around his fractured skull.

'Must have cost ya a pretty penny.' Hawkins remarked through the steam of his coffee. 'I hear they're worth ten of most saddle horses.'

'Nope. I never paid one red cent for that critter.' the bounty hunter told the two men. 'I done killed me the Mexican that was riding it. A *vaquero* with mighty fine silver thread stitched into his sombrero, as I recall.'

Both Lowe and Hawkins glanced at one another.

Then the sheriff edged closer to the strange man with the even stranger-looking solid bandage around his head. The long hair which hung from beneath the grey skullcap seemed even more bizarre now that the doctor had finished his handiwork. It hung over the broad shoulders and in front of the unseeing eyes like a veil.

'Ya killed the owner of that horse?' Hawkins enquired nervously. 'Any particular reason why ya'd do that, son?'

A twisted smile showed the sharp teeth of the seated bounty hunter.

'Sure I had me a reason for killing that *vaquero*. He was trying to kill me.' Iron Eyes spat the words as though he had just seen the face of the *vaquero* again. 'I come on him all peaceable like and he opened up on me for no reason. Started shooting from up there on the back of that big old palomino as if I was a threat to him or something. Took part of my ear off. So I just shot him. It was a clean kill and worth the two bullets I wasted. That horse gotta be worth more than fourteen cents by anyone's reckoning. Right?'

'Right,' Hawkins agreed. 'Gotta be worth a whole lot more than the price of two bullets.'

'And the horse?' Lowe asked curiously. 'Why'd you take his horse?'

'My pony had died a few hours earlier and I needed a fresh horse, so I just kinda took that un.' Iron Eyes recalled. He lifted the hair away from his ear beneath the cement cap. 'Look at that ear. Wouldn't you have killed someone who done that to you?'

Both men nodded slowly.

'That must have hurt,' Hawkins said.

'Stung a little.' Iron Eyes allowed his mane to drop and cover the old wound. 'It weren't the pain, it was the principle of the thing. Ya can't let folks shoot off ya ears without doing something about it. Can ya?'

'Sure enough,' Lowe agreed.

Iron Eyes rubbed his eyes and blinked hard. His eyes still refused to work. 'When do ya figure I'll be able to see again, Doc? Ya got my head in this damned heavy vice and I still can't see nothing.'

Lowe patted the shoulder of the frustrated man. 'Easy. It'll take as long as it takes. Could come back after you've had a good night's sleep.'

Iron Eyes clenched both hands until the bones of his fists went white as they lay on top of the saddle-bags on his lap. 'I figure that means ya ain't got a clue. I might be blind for keeps and that don't sit well in my craw. Not all outlaws stink as well as Kansas Drew did. I need to be able to see. My life ain't worth a plug nickel otherwise.'

'Fretting ain't gonna make ya heal faster, son,' Hawkins said firmly. 'Patience is a virtue, ya know.'

Iron Eyes tilted his head towards the voice of the lawman. 'I ain't got a clue what the hell ya talking about, Sheriff.'

76

'Tell me, Iron Eyes. What exactly happened to your pony that made it up and die?' Doc Lowe asked. He walked to the enamel basin and started to try and wash the hardened cement from his hands. He added more hot water from the blackened kettle perched on his stove beside the coffee pot and scrubbed his digits feverishly.

'I shot it. That's why he died,' the bounty hunter replied. 'It was spent and I shot it.'

'Reckon that's kinda merciful.' Lowe sighed.

Iron Eyes pulled a cigar from his inside pocket and placed it between his teeth. He struck a match and inhaled the smoke deeply. 'Not really. The damn thing almost killed me when it buckled at full gallop. I kicked it a few times but it wouldn't get up.'

'So ya shot it.' Hawkins finished the sentence and watched a wry smile etch itself across the horrific features of the thin emaciated man seated a few feet from him.

'It was a pretty poor pony to start with,' Iron Eyes recalled. 'I had me a tussle with an Apache who took exception to my face. He didn't need the pony after I killed him.'

'You use them guns of yours a whole lot, boy.' The sheriff topped up his coffee and sat opposite the bounty hunter as he sucked in more of the strong acrid smoke he seemed to savour.

'I only kill things that need killing.' Iron Eyes gripped the cigar between his teeth and then

77

unbuckled the nearer of the saddle-bag satchels. He pulled out a full bottle of whiskey and placed it down on the desk next to his elbow. 'That ought to cover the cost of the bottle of liquor I seem to have drunk, Doc.'

Lowe gave a smile. 'I was gonna just add it to my bill, Iron Eyes. But thank you kindly all the same.'

Iron Eyes turned to the sheriff. 'Kansas Drew was worth a hundred dollars last time I checked, Sheriff. Give that money to Doc here. That ought to settle my debt with some loose change left over.'

Hawkins touched his temple. 'What about them Barton boys? How much are their rotting hides worth?'

'Five hundred for the set.' The bounty hunter sighed. 'I'll have that bounty as soon as this town's bank opens up.'

'Reckon with that much hard cash ya won't be needing to go on after them two other outlaws.' Hawkins said. 'Not for a few weeks anyways.'

A surprised expression covered the face of the man with the cement cap. 'What ya mean?'

'Ain't no call for ya to be chasing them until that head of yours is mended,' the sheriff explained. 'Why risk hurting yourself chasing after them two outlaws?'

'They nearly killed me, Sheriff!' Iron Eyes pulled the cigar from his teeth and blew out a line of smoke at the floor. 'I don't cotton to folks trying to kill me.

Besides they're still wanted dead or alive. I intend collecting that reward money.'

'Let me take ya horse to the livery and have it bedded down for the night, Iron Eyes,' Hawkins said as he took another sip of the strong black coffee. 'You get a room in the hotel and rest up for a while. Maybe when ya eyesight comes back—'

'I don't hanker to be lying in no hotel room blind,' the thin figure snarled through cigar smoke. 'I'll be a target for any half-witted *hombre* who wants to try and kill me.'

Lowe managed at last to free his hands of most of the cement. He dried them on a towel, then he strolled back to the seated man. 'Joe's right, son. There ain't no threat to you in the town no more. Ya killed all the vermin who might have tried to kill you already. Now are ya gonna take a room at the hotel for a few days or not?'

Iron Eyes turned to the medical man. 'Nope. I'm riding out after them two outlaws as soon as I've bin paid my bounty.'

Hawkins and Lowe watched as Iron Eyes withdrew another bottle which only had half its contents remaining. He pulled its cork and started to down the whiskey.

'But that rain will wash their horse tracks clean away, son,' the lawman stated, pointing at the window and the rain which pounded its panes. 'Even if ya could see it's impossible for anyone to find a trail that's bin washed clean away by a storm.'

Iron Eyes lowered the bottle from his twisted lips. 'They can't git away from me, old-timer. I don't need no trail to follow their breed.'

'Ya don't?' Hawkins queried.

The thin trigger finger of the bounty hunter's left hand tapped the side of his nose. 'I'm like an old hound dog. I'll track them by the stink they left.'

'That ain't possible.' Lowe chuckled.

'It is, Doc!' Iron Eyes disagreed. 'Them two outlaws are leaving a scent made from pure fear. I can follow that even with my eyes not working.'

'But what happens if you do catch up with them and ya still can't see?' Lowe asked quietly. 'They might bushwhack ya.'

'They don't know I'm blind, Doc,' Iron Eyes said in a low, cold tone which chilled both the other two men. 'All they know is that the same man who killed their three partners is following. They're gutless and I ain't.'

Hawkins slammed his mug down angrily. 'For heaven's sake. Ya blind, Iron Eyes. Face the facts. Without rest like Doc recommends that might be permanent. Do ya want to be blind for ever?'

Iron Eyes downed another long swallow and then rested the bottle on top of the saddle-bags on his lap.

'My horse can see. He'll get me to where I need to go and then all I gotta do is shoot them.'

'It's suicidal,' Lowe whispered into the ear of his

friend the sheriff. Hawkins nodded in silent agreement.

Iron Eyes continued to drink his whiskey and stare through the blood-soaked strands of his matted hair with eyes which refused to see.

Frustrated, Sheriff Hawkins turned away from the defiant bounty hunter and glanced up at the wall clock. There was still seven hours left before sunup. He faced the window as another blinding flash of lightning lit up the streets of San Remo. He rubbed his neck and looked over his shoulder.

'You'll die, Iron Eyes. All because ya damn stubborn.'

'We're all gonna die, Sheriff.' Iron Eyes sighed. 'Maybe it's best if'n ya can't see it coming.'

NINE

The previous night's storm had not slowed them. They feared what lay behind them far more than the rods of lightning which had exploded all around their bedraggled forms. Yet neither Whip Slater or Clem Barker had ever ventured into a place so fearsome as the forested valley before. All their gun skills were of no use in such primitive surroundings. The creatures that killed here did not require artificial assistance to achieve their bloody goals. Sharp claws and teeth were a match for bullets in this uncharted land. The forest held a million unseen dangers that neither man knew anything about. They were like children here, children faced with something potentially lethal yet beyond their comprehension. The dense brush which obstructed almost every gap between the countless tree trunks emitted sounds along the length of the valley such as neither rider had ever heard before. The growls of bears and the nerve-shattering sound of large cats hung over both outlaws as the true vastness of this place became clear to them. They were out of their depth but fear kept them going: fear of the bounty hunter they knew would not rest until he had added them to his tally.

This was no border town main street with the sound of guitars and pianos filling the air. This was a wild land which looked as though no two-legged creature had ever ventured into it before. But the totem poles told a different story. Totem poles marked the length of the river as if declaring ownership. Neither Slater nor Barker had seen them until the sun had risen.

Now it was far too late to do anything but continue on their long ride. Silently both outlaws wondered whether the people who had carved these tall wooden totems still dwelled in the forested valley.

During the hours of darkness both riders had skimmed the bank of the river on their journey. Now as the first rays of a new dawn began to illuminate everything which surrounded them they slowly started to realize that they might have made a mistake.

This was no ordinary short cut they were travelling along astride their weary mounts. This was something far more dangerous. Both men's heads darted from side to side as one sound after another rose up as their horses walked in the cold fast-flowing water which raced back to where they had started their journey. Each sound was unknown to them. Each sound heralded their arrival to all the other creatures who lay hidden under the carpet of lush greenery which stretched away on all sides.

Slater had looked back many times since sunup. There was no trace of the place where they had come from. Only tall trees, rising up to the very heavens, met his tired eyes. And the totem poles.

Barker looked ahead and to both sides as he led the way. His nerves were shot but he refused to allow his partner to see his barely contained terror. The low mist ahead of them seemed to hang in the air like the spirits of long dead people. There was no wind here to dispel the eerie clouds. No wind at all.

Both outlaws knew that however dangerous this valley was it was nothing to the peril which lay behind them. They had seen how Iron Eyes dispatched his venom. How he collected his bounty money. His blood money. There were no sweet words from the thin man dressed in the garb of an undertaker. He did not attempt to bring his victims in alive even though he had that option. To Iron Eyes dead or alive simply meant dead.

The vision of the ruthless hunter of men had kept both men spurring their horses during the entire length of the long dark night. The valley with its unknown creatures could not hold a candle to the terrifying image of Iron Eyes.

Again both men spurred their spent horses.

'How far we gotta ride, Whip?' Barker asked over his shoulder. 'We gotta be close to reaching the end of this damn valley, ain't we?'

Slater drew his horse level with his companion. He rubbed his whiskered face and glanced at the slightly younger outlaw. 'I ain't sure, but I figure it'll take us another couple of days to get to clear ground and Providence.'

Barker's head swung to look straight at Slater. 'What? We gotta keep riding through here for another couple of days? I ain't happy about that. Nope. I sure ain't.'

'Ya wanna turn back?' Slater shouted across the short distance between them. 'We bin riding for maybe eight hours or more and that's a lot of ground to cover. We have to just keep going.'

'I don't like the look of them totem poles, Whip,' Barker said, pointing as they passed yet another. 'In the dark I figured they was trees but they ain't trees. Damn it all, they ain't trees!'

'They just mean that there used to be Injuns along here.' Slater said, trying to convince himself that there was nothing to worry about. 'Look at them. Rotten. I reckon the folks that made 'em are long dead.'

More strange sounds echoed about the two horse-men. It was impossible to tell where the sounds originated or what had made them. Barker cleared his throat.

'What was that noise, Whip?' he croaked. 'A bear maybe, or a puma? Huh? We could be heading towards a pack of wolves for all we knows. I don't cotton to this damn place. Injuns! I bet it's a whole tribe of them sending messages to each other about us. I bet they're planning to hang our scalps on their war lances already.'

'Will ya quit babbling?' Slater pleaded and sighed. He was as confused and as frightened as his pal but it did not appear to show so readily. 'I figure we got us enough fire power between us to kill any critter that might get close, Clem. OK?'

'I'm going loco here.' Barker pulled back on his reins. His horse stopped and dropped its head to the fresh water. 'I'm tuckered out, Whip. Me and my horse both. We gotta get us some shut-eye. I can't think no more.'

Slater eased his own horse to a halt and looked back at Barker. He studied the surrounding trees. He nodded. 'Ya right, Clem. We need to sleep and get the weight off these horses' backs. They'll drop for sure if we keep pushing them ahead the way we bin doing. While we sleep they can rest and graze.'

Barker looked around them again. So many bushes and so many trees. It felt as though a thousand eyes were watching their every move. The sounds of the forested teased their ears again. 'I figure we oughta sleep in turns, Whip. Anything could creep up on us if we was both sleeping.'

Again Slater nodded. 'Ya right.'

Both men dismounted cautiously. Their tired eyes darted about at every little noise that came out of the green brush all around them.

The floor of the forest had not seen much of the storm which had passed over the mountains and the valley during the long hours of darkness. The river had swollen only slightly as both outlaws led their horses away from the water's edge to a line of saplings.

'We'll bed down here.' Slater pointed as he lifted his stirrup and fender and began to unhitch his cinch. 'These young trees will guard our backs.'

Barker looked beyond the saplings. Whatever lay further away from the place where they stood was shrouded in blackness. 'Ya sure this is a safe spot, Whip? Might be wild critters in there just waiting to kill and eat us.'

Slater hauled his saddle off the back of his horse and laid down. He looped his reins around the horn of the saddle and secured them firmly. 'Let 'em eat me. I'm too damn tired to care.'

Barker pulled his own saddle off the back of his mount. Steam rose into the air. 'These horses need rubbing down.'

Slater untied his bedroll, spread it out, then lay down upon it, pulling the brim of his Stetson over his eyes. 'Good notion, Clem. You up and rub the horses down while I get some sleep.'

'That ain't fair.'

'Nothing in this damn life of ours is fair, Clem.' Slater yawned. 'I'd've thought that you'd have worked that out by now.'

Barker tossed his bedroll on the ground next to Slater and kicked it until it unfolded. 'Damn the horses. I'm gonna git me some shut-eye.'

Silently Whip Slater reached for his holstered gun and quietly pulled it free. He rested the Colt Frontier .45 on his belly.

If anything came within a gunshot of where he lay, the outlaw was going to kill it.

The storm had achieved one thing. It had washed and blown the dust off San Remo. Yet for three of the people within the confines of the sprawling settlement there was something else on their minds. Iron Eyes remained seated on the chair next to the cluttered desk, sipping on what remained of his last bottle of whiskey, whilst the elderly doctor slept on his couch. As the wall clock chimed Joe Hawkins moved to the bounty hunter and grabbed the bottle from the bony hands.

'Gimme some of that rotgut, boy,' the sheriff said. He lifted the bottle to his lips and took a long swallow of the fiery liquid. Then he sighed and returned the bottle to its owner. 'Damn! That's good whiskey, Iron Eyes.'

The bounty hunter tilted his head back. 'What

time is it?'

Hawkins glanced at the clock. 'Nine.'

'The bank open yet?' Iron Eyes lifted the bottle and drained the remaining droplets of whiskey into his mouth. 'I figure ya ought to be headed off there getting my money, Sheriff.'

The lawman rubbed the back of his neck and walked to the window to survey the street and the dozens of people who now walked along it. 'It don't open for another thirty minutes, but I'll go and rustle up the manager and get what ya owed.'

Iron Eyes stood and carefully placed the bottle down on the desk top. He then strode to the sheriff's side and placed a hand on the shorter man's shoulder.

'I'll go with ya.'

'OK. C'mon.' Hawkins opened the office door and led his companion out into the fresh air. Everything smelled clean. That surprised both men as they walked along the boardwalk in the direction of the bank.

Even blind, the tall thin man could sense the fear his appearance aroused in those who saw his ghostly appearance. With the crude but effective cement cast on his skull he knew that he must be an even more horrific sight.

'Folks are sure skittish in this town, Sheriff.'

'Do ya blame them, boy?' Hawkins chuckled as he carefully guided the bounty hunter towards the bank

89

and its unsuspecting manager. 'Ya ain't the prettiest thing ever to ride into San Remo.'

Iron Eyes turned his head and listened intently. He could hear the voices of those who were genuinely terrified by what they saw.

'How far?'

Hawkins helped the tall figure up on to the raised boardwalk outside the bank, then paused. 'Here we are. Ya coming in or are ya staying out here?'

Iron Eyes turned to face the street. It was as though he were searching for anyone who might be foolish enough to claw back on their gun hammer and take a quick shot at him.

'Reckon I'll just stand here and scare a few folks.'

The sheriff tapped on the glass of the door until he was allowed to enter. For what seemed an eternity the bounty hunter just stood like a statue outside the bank. For all that time not one person came close to him. They all moved out across the street in order to give him a wide berth.

Iron Eyes pulled a cigar from his pocket and placed it between his teeth. He chewed.

Slater and Barker had rested for as long as they dared. Both men had resaddled their horses and mounted. It was now nearly noon; the sun was directly over the valley but neither man noticed. All either of them could think of was the sound which they had both just heard. Slater held his reins tightly and looked up the long river to where he thought he had heard something. His eyes searched vainly for a sign of what might lie up there beyond the bend in the river.

'I heard me something, Clem,' Slater said. 'Did you hear it?'

Barker paused. 'Yep. What you figure it was?'

Slater shook his head. 'Sounded like dynamite to me.'

'That's what I figured, but who'd be using explosives here?' Barker leaned back and pulled his Winchester from its scabbard beneath his saddle. He cocked the rifle and then rested it across his lap next to the saddle horn. 'Reckon we ought to reconsider us turning back, Whip?'

'Hush the hell up,' Slater said. 'I ain't in no mood to start thinking about running away from nothing.'

'If someone is using dynamite up yonder I for one don't reckon it's Injuns.' Barker said. 'But that might not be a good thing. We might be headed towards a whole bunch of real ornery white folks who don't like trespassers.'

Slater checked his gun. 'Let's go see who it is making all that noise, Clem.'

Another muffled blast came down river. Both horses spooked beneath their masters, making it necessary for the outlaws to steady them.

'What's going on up there?'

'Whoever they are, if they start something I'm

91

ready.' Barker patted his rifle and then tapped his spurs. The two outlaws rode towards where they had heard the muffled sounds. 'I'm ready to kill anyone or anything, Whip. My back hurts and I'm busting for a fight.'

Slater took a deep breath. 'Yeah. It's gotta be better than going backwards to run into that Iron Eyes bastard. Facing dynamite ain't as bad as facing up to that critter. C'mon. Whoever it is making that ruckus upriver, we'll kill 'em.'

'If'n they don't kill us first,' Barker said. He raised himself in his stirrups and urged his horse on.

The weary outlaws headed along the edge of the fast-flowing river toward the place where the mist hung low above the water.

Neither of the riders realized that what lay ahead of them was quite as dangerous as what they feared behind them.

TEN

A lonely stagecoach was led out from the livery stables across the wide street from where the sheriff stood as the doors of the bank were locked behind him. The lawman glanced up from the handful of cash in his hands as two stablemen controlled the six-horse team whilst the driver climbed up to his high perch. Hawkins then cast his eyes to the side to where the lonely figure of the bounty hunter stood. The thin man had not moved more than a few inches since Hawkins had left him on the boardwalk. The man with the tin star pinned to his vest walked to the side of the hideous Iron Eyes and cleared his throat.

'I know ya there, Sheriff,' Iron Eyes drawled as his left hand rose to the cement skullcap for the umpteenth time.

'Reckon ya do.'

Iron Eyes lowered his arm and showed the palm of his hand to the sherff. Hawkins obliged by putting the reward money into its dry grip.

The sheriff pulled his pipe from his pocket and chewed on its stem thoughtfully. He still could not understand the thin figure beside him, but he knew that whatever Iron Eyes was, he was dangerous. He was also deadly even when blind.

'Ya coming back to the office?' Hawkins asked. 'Doc might have a fresh pot of coffee on the stove by now.'

'That don't thrill me too much.' Iron Eyes held the cash in his left hand as the other one rested on the sheriff's shoulder.

Both men were silent as they headed back to the small building where Doc Lowe still slept. As they reached the corner of the alley the bounty hunter stopped and turned his head. He stepped down on to the dusty street, moved away from the lawman and towards the big palomino stallion.

'Can ya see now, boy?' Hawkins asked as he followed the tall figure to where the horse and its master stood. 'Has ya sight come back?'

Iron Eyes stroked the neck of the horse. 'Nope. I can't see nothing at all, Sheriff.'

Hawkins stood beside the strange man. 'Ya caught the horse's scent? Is that how ya knew where he was?'

'Nope,' Iron Eyes replied. 'I heard him snorting. He's got a temper and being left out in a storm all night has just fired him up. He's real angry with me right now.'

'I never heard him snort,' the law officer admitted. 'I figured it's because ya eyes ain't working that ya other senses are working better.'

Iron Eyes patted the stallion's neck and turned to Hawkins. 'Maybe. I like to keep him ornery, Sheriff. He's a damn good horse but he's better when he's got a beef with me.'

Hawkins patted the shoulder of the bounty hunter. 'Let me take him to the stables and get him rubbed down, boy. There ain't no way that ya can ride out until them eyes of yours are working again. Let the horse rest.'

The man with the gruesome face turned his head quickly. Even though his eyes could not see, they burned like fiery torches straight into the soul of the lawman. 'What? Are ya deaf or just forgetful? I told ya I was riding out when I got me my blood money. That's what I'm gonna do. I'm riding.'

'But this is madness, son,' Hawkins protested vainly. 'I know that ya the famed Iron Eyes. The man that they say can't be killed but ya can be killed. Them outlaws will be out there waiting someplace for ya and they'll finish ya off. Mark my words, Iron Eyes, they'll kill ya.'

Iron Eyes gripped the sheriff's shoulder and squeezed hard. His bony fingers dug deep. 'I'm not scared of no vermin. Anyways, how can they kill me? I'm already dead, old-timer. Ask anyone. I'm dead! Ya can't kill a dead man.'

The two men walked away from the stallion, stepped up on to the boardwalk and a few paces later entered the office. Lowe was still snoring on his leather couch. Hawkins closed the door and studied the bounty hunter closely. He watched as the thin fingers peeled off a few of the bills and slid them into his pants pocket. The rest of the bounty money he placed on the desk beside the empty whiskey bottles.

'What ya doing?' the sheriff asked.

'Leaving the money with old Doc,' came the swift reply.

'Why? I already got Doc's fee from the bounty on that Kansas Drew critter ya gunned down.'

'Safe keeping,' Iron Eyes muttered.

'Safe keeping? Ya intending heading back this way to pick up the money, boy?' Hawkins could not understand the motives of this strange man. He was bewildered.

'I doubt it.'

Hawkins looked at the money as the bills slowly unfolded on the pile of papers cluttered on the desk. There were hundreds of dollars there. 'Are ya giving ya bounty money away, boy? Why hunt down outlaws and give most of the reward money away to a stranger? It don't make no sense.'

'I got me more than enough money for the horse's feed and my whiskey and bullets, Sheriff.' Iron Eyes said drily. 'I don't need the rest at the moment. Money slows me down. Blunts my edge and makes me kinda sluggish.'

'But what if ya need more money?'

'Then I'll just kill me a few more outlaws.' Iron Eyes grinned a crooked grin. 'Only the ones wanted dead, that is.'

'That skull of yours must have bin busted even worse than I figured,' Hawkins opined. 'Ya give ya money away and decide to keep chasing outlaws even though ya as blind as a bat. Yep! I figure ya brain must have bin mashed up like a pot of sweet potatoes.'

Iron Eyes exhaled loudly. 'I'm a hunter, Sheriff. Always bin a hunter. It's all I know. How to kill.'

Hawkins moved to the doctor and shook him with both hands. Lowe's eyes opened. He looked at the two men in his office and smiled. The lawman turned back to face the bounty hunter.

'I don't understand you at all, boy,' the sheriff admitted.

Iron Eyes sat down again in the chair he had polished with his pants seat during the night. He extracted one of the bills and waved it at the lawman. 'Here.'

'I don't take bribes.'

'This ain't no damn bribe. It's to go and buy us three steak dinners and have 'em brung here,' Iron Eyes stated. His left hand slid down to the neck of his boot and drew out his honed Bowie knife.'

'What ya doing with that knife, boy?' the sheriff

cautiously asked the seated figure who seemed to be weighing the weapon in his right hand.

Iron Eyes turned his face towards Hawkins. 'Ya said I was as blind as a bat and couldn't go riding off without getting myself killed, old-timer. right?'

'Right enough.'

'Throw something at that far wall,' the bounty hunter drawled. 'Anything at all.'

The sheriff was about to argue when he decided it might be better if he complied with the request. Hawkins wanted to try and prove to the wounded man that he was not fit enough to ride out of San Remo. His fingers searched his vest pocket and produced a silver dollar.

'Will a dollar do?'

Iron Eyes slowly nodded as he listened to the coin being tossed and caught by the lawman. 'It'll do just fine.'

'Here goes.' Hawkins dropped his hand and tossed the coin across the room. Before the coin had reached the tobacco-stained wall the bounty hunter slung the large knife at full force. The tip of the knife's blade hit the coin, then embedded itself in the wall.

'What you doing?' Doc Lowe asked sleepily.

Iron Eyes smiled. 'Proving a point. I ain't as helpless as our star-packing pal here thinks.'

Joe Hawkins walked to the knife, pulled it from the wall and scooped up his coin. The knife's tip had scarred its silver surface. Silently he strode back to the bounty hunter and exchanged the hefty weapon for the twenty-dollar bill. 'So ya can hit a coin with a knife.'

'I can also shoot folks dead,' Iron Eyes added. 'Ask Kansas Drew McGinty if that ain't a fact.'

'Are you sure you can't see?' Hawkins growled, waving his hands in front of the blank eyes of the seated man.

'Not a damn thing, old-timer.'

Hawkins sighed heavily. 'Incredible!'

'I'm gonna ride on out of this town after I've had me some vittles and filled my saddle-bags with whiskey bottles,' the bounty hunter said. He slid the knife back down into his boot. 'Maybe my sight will return before I catch up with them outlaws.'

Hawkins shook his head. 'I got me a feeling it will.'

'Damn right, old-timer. Now go get us them steak meals,' Iron Eyes said. 'And some whiskey. Don't forget the bottles of whiskey.'

'If I weren't so hungry I might not be willing to run errands for a ruthless bounty hunter,' Hawkins observed. 'But a steak would go down real well just now.'

It was a confused Doc Lowe who stared at the pile of cash on his desk. He scratched his head and pulled out the chair next to where his patient was seated. The lawman left the office, walked out into the busy street and headed towards the café.

Lowe sat down next to his patient and looked at the cement bandage carefully. 'How'd ya feel?'

The ghostlike creature turned towards the doctor. His face seemed expressionless. 'A whole lot better if I could see ya again, Doc,' he said.

'You seem to be doing pretty good without being able to see, my boy.' Lowe smiled.

Iron Eyes buried his face into his hands. 'Don't be fooled so easy, Doc. It's all bin tricks. Just a whole heap of damn tricks.'

ELEVEN

The forest got darker the deeper the two outlaws rode into its depths. The bottom of the most fearsome ocean could never have created more demons than those which fermented like rotgut whiskey in their imaginations. Slater and Barker had been drawn like moths to a flame by their curiosity and the need to get to the end of this frightening place. The sounds of explosions had grown louder the further they rode up into the valley of trees. The mist hung lower over the river until it was as though they had entered the belly of a cloud.

Then, as they rounded a bend, all fell silent.

Nothing stirred. Now only the pounding of their racing hearts filled their ears.

Slater drew rein and kept the leathers up under his chin as his eyes vainly searched the area that lay ahead of them. Barker allowed his horse to drink whilst he nursed his Winchester and also studied the terrain.

'I don't like it,' Slater admitted.

'Whatever it was that bin making all the noise has quit, Whip,' Barker observed.

Slater relaxed slightly, released the grip of his right hand and lowered his arm until his gloved fingers were above the pearl-handled gun on his hip.

'Yeah, whoever it was has gone kinda coy,' the horseman remarked nervously. The outlaw then looked up and saw what appeared to be smoke drifting across the expanse of fast-moving water. He pointed. 'The blasts must have come from up yonder, by my reckoning.'

Barker teased his mount forward until both animals were shoulder to shoulder. He moved the long-barrelled weapon around, as if daring whatever it had been that had been making the explosions to appear.

'I got me a bad feeling about this, Whip.'

'You and me both, Clem.' Slater nodded as he slid his gun from its holster and pulled back on its hammer. He rested the pistol on his thigh and turned his head slightly. There was another bend just 200 yards from where their horses stood. 'I figure we bin spotted. That's why they stopped blasting.'

Barker sighed. It was a heavy sigh created by fear of the unknown. He had been in many scrapes during his short but fruitful career as an outlaw but nothing had ever scared him quite as much as this valley.

'Who do ya figure it was using explosives? And why? There ain't no mining camps that I've seen.'

Slater looked at yet another totem pole. It was rotten, as the water lapped like a thirsty cat at its base. He rubbed his dry mouth along his sleeve.

'I ain't sure about nothing any more. All I keep thinking about is them damn totem poles. We could be surrounded by a whole bunch of redskins and not know it.'

'Injuns ain't got no black powder or dynamite,' Barker said through gritted teeth. 'Ya said that yourself. What we got to be wary of is white critters. White critters that can blow us into a million pieces.'

'Yeah,' Slater muttered. His eyes continued to search for whatever or whoever it might be who dwelled in the dense forest and played with deadly explosives.

'Right now I'd prefer to run into a whole tribe of Injuns, pal,' Barker croaked. 'I don't hanker to have myself blown apart by some loco prospectors.'

Suddenly above them through the swirling mist they heard a strange sound. It was the noise of movement. But a noise unlike anything either rider had ever heard before.

Both looked up at the same moment. They saw the wires which had been stretched across the river in various directions and before either of them could utter a word their eyes noticed them start to vibrate.

A sickening humming filled the air.

'What in tarnation is that?'

'What's going on?'

Whip Slater steadied his horse as it too became as nervous as its master. 'Wish the hell I knew, Clem.'

The mist began to stir as if it was alive. It curled and moved as the wires which ran through it shook the very air itself over their heads. Something was coming. They both sensed it. They could hear it. But what? What was coming?

Then another series of sounds filled their ears. This time it was on the ground. Their eyes widened as all around them the brush began to heave as bushes appeared to come to life and move towards them.

'What the hell?' Barker almost screamed as he felt his mount buck beneath his saddle. The outlaw's hand let go of the rifle barrel and grabbed at his reins. He fought the animal into submission. 'Easy, boy. Easy.'

'The brush is alive, Clem,' Slater yelled.

'What we damn well ridden into, Whip?' Barker gasped as he managed to bring his rifle back up into his shaking hands. 'Is we dead? Have we bin running scared from Iron Eyes and ended up riding into Hell?'

Nervously Slater raised his gun and trained it on the moving bushes. He did not know what to do. His trigger finger wanted to squeeze and kill but his mind could not see how he could kill bushes. 'This place is haunted, Clem.'

Barker eventually steadied his mount. 'There ain't no such animal as ghosts, Whip.'

Whip Slater fired at the bushes. 'Whatever that is I'm gonna kill it.'

The air filled with acrid gunsmoke as both outlaws fired their weaponry at the approaching bushes. Then above them the humming noise grew louder. Again the outlaws' attention was drawn to the wires that buzzed like a hive of crazed hornets. To their utter shock they saw something moving from beyond the low-hanging mist. Neither had seen such a sight before and shock showed in their ashen faces.

'What is it?' Barker yelled out.

'A bird?' Slater ventured.

'It's a man!'

The eerie sight came across the river at speed. It broke through the low cloud on its journey towards them. Faster and faster it came at them. Then as both Slater and Barker raised their weapons at the strange flying object they heard the unmistakable sound of guns being cocked from within the moving bushes.

'Guns.' Barker shouted as he swung his mount around to again face the bushes he and his companion had fired at. His eyes widened as he saw the gun barrels aimed at them. 'Look out, Whip.'

The outlaws had barely had time to focus when the

weapons of the men hidden behind the bushes unleashed their fury.

'This is a damn bushwhackin', Clem,' Slater shouted at his partner as he tried to swing his skittish horse around.

Before Barker could respond he felt the power of the bullets cut into him. The impact almost sent him flying over his cantle. Only his stirrups, which held his boots in check, kept the outlaw on his mount. 'I bin hit.'

Gunsmoke curled and twisted as more and more red-hot lead spewed out at them. The barrage of artillery came fast and furious. Slater tried to return fire but his gun was empty and then he too was rocked by the bullets that punched into his body. He swayed like a prize fighter on the ropes.

Defying his own agony, Barker managed to level his rifle and return two last shots. Then he buckled as another volley of lead cut into him. His horse swung full circle as the flying object over their heads reached them both. Will Hayes raised his boots and kicked both men in turn. Slater and Barker flew from their mounts and crashed into the muddy ground.

Barker got to his feet quickly and started to shoot in all directions. It was the last act of a man whose entire body was riddled with bullet wounds. Blood poured from him as the outlaw finally fell back on to his knees and then crumpled. The outlaw gave out a last gasp as his face sank into the soft wet ground.

Slater lay on his back. His finger kept pulling on the trigger of his gun but there were no more bullets in its chambers. Hayes drew and fired his gun and finished the doomed man.

Then, like a pack of wolves, the miners rushed out from their hiding-places. They swarmed over the lifeless bodies and made sure the men were dead. Another half-dozen shots rang out as the master magician released himself from his rigging and dropped down to his men.

'They're dead.' Hayes yelled out. 'Quit shooting.'

Bob Tobey and the rest of the men ceased their mindless firing at the bullet-ridden corpses.

'Grab them horses,' Hayes ordered. 'That's what we wanted. Their horses.'

The miners did as they were told. Henson walked to where Hayes stood with one of the horses, a broad smile wreathing his features. 'Ya was right, Will. Them two varmints come like a bear to a honey pot.'

'Two good strong horses,' Rance Bean noted. 'Reckon they'll be able to carry a whole lot of gold out of here, boys.'

'I knew that the sound of small explosions would either frighten them away or draw them into my trap, boys,' Hayes said, nodding. 'Now we got us two more horses to carry our spoils out of this forest.'

Pete Brown had carefully checked both bodies for

any clues to their identities. He stood with blood-covered hands and stepped over what remained of the outlaws. He rubbed the gore off on his clothing and spat at the ground.

'These critters had no papers on them.'

Hayes paced to the dead men, placed his knuckles on his hips and stared down at their handiwork. 'Good! I reckon they ain't gonna be missed. Most important folks got something with their names on it. These are just saddle tramps, I reckon. No one will ever miss them.'

'They had a few bucks between them,' Brown added. 'Nothing more.'

Sly Rowe pushed his smoking gun back into its holster. 'We gonna bury them, Will?'

Hayes shook his head. 'Nah, just kick their bloody carcasses into the river, boys. Let the river dispose of them.'

A cheerless laughter erupted from the six men.

The miners did as they were instructed and kicked the lifeless bodies over the muddy ground into the river. It did not take long before the strong current dragged them out into the white water. They watched the two bodies being washed downriver with a cruel, heartless satisfaction.

But as they watched the remains of the luckless men disappearing in the waves none of them had any idea that other eyes were also observing them.

Eyes which now knew the truth.

Hakatan had seen the men who masqueraded as gods unmasked.

Silently he stepped back into the shadows.

TWELVE

No caged animal could have shown as much fury as Iron Eyes. The tall man was angry. Not with the countless outlaws he had faced during his bloody past but angry with something he did not comprehend. Doc Lowe watched silently as the bounty hunter paced around the confines of his small office like a puma trying to find a means of escape. The old doctor knew that there were no words which could calm the fearsome hunter of men. Nothing he could either say or do could restore the sight of a man who by rights ought to be dead. Time and luck were the only things which might bring back the sight to the bullet-coloured eyes. But Iron Eyes was not a man to wait.

Panic had overwhelmed the man with the pair of deadly Navy Colts jutting from his pants belt. Panic at realizing that he might actually never see again. To a hunter who relied on all his honed senses to outwit and kill his prey it meant that his life was virtually over.

Iron Eyes was blind. At last he had admitted it to himself. Chairs had been upturned as the thin creature had bumped into them in his fury of frustration. What burned the hottest inside Iron Eyes was the fact that he was helpless.

Helpless to do anything but wait.

As he crashed into the desk for the umpteenth time Lowe's small, weathered hand grabbed at his long black frock-coat and stopped him.

Iron Eyes was panting like a hound. He paused and grabbed at the cement cast which surrounded his fractured skull and snarled. 'Let go, Doc.'

'Sit down.'

'I don't wanna sit down,' Iron Eyes raged, clenching both fists. 'I wanna see! Ya might as well put a bullet through my skull if I'm blind.'

Lowe released his feeble grip. 'What about them tricks ya was telling about, boy? Mighty fine tricks if I'm any judge. Ya managed to use ya hearing to outgun that McGinty critter. Ya even managed to hit that silver dollar Joe tossed in the air, with ya knife. Them tricks, as ya call them, are skills, boy. I could live to be a hundred and I couldn't better them.'

Iron Eyes began to calm down. 'But I gotta be able to see.'

'And you will.' Lowe's voice was reassuring.

Iron Eyes felt himself being guided into the chair

next to the older man. He fumbled in his pocket and produced a cigar and match.

'When?'

'That I can't be certain of, son,' Lowe said.

Iron Eyes ran a thumbnail over the top of the match. It erupted into flame. He sucked in the smoke and threw his head back. He winced in pain for a few seconds.

'What's wrong?' Lowe asked.

'My head hurt,' came the resigned reply. 'It's OK now. When's that lawman gonna get back here?'

Lowe looked out of the window at the street beyond. It was bathed in sunshine. 'He said he was taking ya horse to be fed and watered.'

'That was hours back.' Iron Eyes blew a line of smoke at the ceiling. 'He shouldn't have bothered. I told him that horse is better when he's ornery.'

Lowe sipped at his coffee and leaned back on his chair. He watched the quiet figure who chewed on the acrid black cigar thoughtfully. The cement head-guard was crude but it seemed to be working, he thought. It was holding Iron Eyes' shattered skull together and that was all that mattered.

Lowe looked at the money his patient had placed on the desk. 'I was wondering about that money. How come you ain't pocketed it, boy?'

'I got me all I need.' Iron Eyes leaned back. 'Money makes a bounty hunter soft. I gotta be sharp like my knife if'n I'm gonna survive. You keep it.'

The older man placed his cup down next to the money and picked the bills up. He had never seen so much money at one time before. 'I don't need it. Take it now.'

'It's yours,' Iron Eyes growled.

'If ya sure?'

'I'm sure.'

Lowe cleared his throat and then pushed the money into his pants pocket. 'Then I thank ya kindly.'

Suddenly Iron Eyes blinked hard and long and then aimed his sightless eyes at the weathered old man. 'My eyes are burning like fury, Doc. Is that normal?'

The doctor stood and carefully placed his hands on the bounty hunter's face. He squinted hard into the bullet-coloured eyes and gave out a sound similar to ones he had made as he ate his dinner. 'This might just be a good sign, boy. A mighty good sign.'

Iron Eyes listened to the doctor as he walked across the room to his cabinet. 'Where ya going?'

'I got me some drops in here which might help.' Lowe answered. 'Might be that them eyes of yours are starting to come to life again. Maybe that brain of yours is starting to wake up again and send out its messages to ya eyes.'

The thin figure remained seated as Doc Lowe closed the cabinet door and returned to his side.

'Ya mean I'll be able to see again soon?'

'I'd not bet against it.' Cautiously Lowe positioned the bounty hunter's head to lean back, and pulled down on one of the lower lids. 'Don't move. I'm gonna put a few drops of this stuff in each of ya eyes. It might sting but it'll help.'

Iron Eyes felt the drops going into both eyes in turn and then felt the stinging. He closed his eyes and gritted his teeth, but he refused to utter any sound.

'I told ya it would sting,' Lowe said as he sat down again.

'My eyes are on fire, Doc. What was that stuff? Snake oil?'

'That's a good sign,' Lowe said hesitantly. 'I think that the nerves are starting to come back to life.'

Iron Eyes opened his eyes and blinked hard. His expression gave nothing away to the old man.

'Well?' Doc Lowe enquired.

'Damn it all. I can see a dim light,' the bounty hunter said. He rose to his full height and stared towards the front of the office. 'I can see the sunlight out there. Nothing clear but I can see something.'

Lowe clapped his hands together. 'We're on the mend, son!'

Iron Eyes was lured to the front of the office by the blurred images out in the street. He found the door handle and opened the door. He stood staring out as he saw the blurred ghostly images of two horses and a man approaching him.

'That you, Sheriff?' Iron Eyes questioned.

'Yep,' Hawkins replied as he stood below the boardwalk. In his hands he held the reins not only of the palomino stallion but his own sturdy saddle horse. 'I brung the horses.'

The bounty hunter tilted his head.

'Horses?'

'I'm tagging along with ya, son,' Hawkins said firmly.

'Why?'

'Ain't too sure.' The sheriff looped the reins around the hitching pole and secured them. 'Reckon I figured that ya might need the help of a fat old man. Until them eyes of yours start working again, that is.'

A twisted smile came to the face of Iron Eyes. 'Ya get the whiskey, old-timer?'

'Five bottles.' Hawkins pushed the brim of his Stetson off his face. 'And some jerky.'

'Jerky, huh?' Iron Eyes cautiously stepped down to the street. 'I'll stick to the whiskey.'

'Suits me.' The sheriff scratched his cheek.

'Let's ride!'

THIRTEEN

Darkness had returned to the forest. The well-disguised miners had deliberately waited until sundown before returning to the camp for fear that too much daylight would betray them. Yet they had already been seen by the one member of the tribe who had the power and will to take his revenge. Hakatan knew the truth about the men who had viciously beaten and killed his people whilst pretending to be reincarnations of their ancient gods. The jubilant miners led the outlaws' horses back into the camp to join their other animals. For some moments none of them noticed anything wrong but that was soon to alter when Will Hayes realized that the large bonfire set between the large building and the smaller ones had not been lit.

The master illusionist paused by the entrance to the gold-filled wigwam as the five others walked in his wake. Hayes raised a hand. The others stopped and turned to look where his masked face was staring.

'What's wrong, Will?' Tobey asked.

'Them natives ain't fired up the bonfire,' Hayes said, his thoat dry.

One by one the miners all turned and looked to the large mound of kindling. Since their first encounter with the reclusive Indians they had never seen the camp shrouded in darkness before.

Hayes walked a few steps away from the entrance. His eyes studied the small huts which dotted the entire area. Eventually it dawned upon him that they were all empty.

'Where are they?' Hayes asked fearfully.

'I got me a feeling things ain't right.' Rowe was first to cock his rifle and rest it against his hip as the others followed suit.

Hayes swallowed hard and cast his mask aside. 'They can't be far. We oughta go round 'em up and make sure they keep doing what we tell 'em to do.'

The others all agreed, with the exception of Clint Henson, who moved to their leader's side. 'I'm for us heading out right now, Will. I reckon them Injuns are gonna hit us hard.'

Hayes rubbed his whiskered chin thoughtfully. 'Ya reckon, Clint? Maybe they all just run off.'

Henson shook his head. 'Nope. Somehow I think they've figured out that we ain't what they thought we was. It might just be payback time.'

'How?' Hayes asked a little alarmed.

'Clint's right.' Rance Bean walked out from the others. He had heard something and trained his Winchester in the direction of the sound. 'We oughta start packing them animals with gold before trouble does come looking for us.'

Hayes did not know what to do. For the first time in his life he was quite at a loss. 'What ya looking at, Rance?'

Bean raised his rifle and aimed into the depths of the undergrowth. 'There's something out there.'

Will Hayes turned and was about to address the others when he heard a sound that chilled him to the bone. There was nothing like the noise a spinning tomahawk made as it cut through the air in pursuit of its chosen target. Hayes spun on his heels just as the Indian hatchet hit Bean in the middle of his broad chest. The miner staggered. His rifle fired into the ground and then he fell into the mud.

The startled men looked up and saw the painted faces in the trees.

The pitiful remnants of the remaining Indians had returned with Hakatan at their head.

The elderly brave gave out a spine-chilling call. Although the miners did not understand a word of the strange language they knew exactly what Hakatan meant.

He had just declared war.

FOURTEEN

Only the light of the moon and stars illuminated the camp as the battle progressed on for what seemed like an eternity to the trapped five remaining false gods. Blistering rounds of awesome force erupted from their rifle barrels as the prospectors who huddled just inside the entrance to the large wigwam kept on shooting. Arrows already riddled its walls and continued flying from all directions straight and true towards them. Will Hayes knelt beside his younger cronies and desperately tried to work out what their next move should be. Yet for all his prowess as a magician, Hayes was unable to think of a trick which would bring their attackers to their knees. He could not understand why the naive natives had revolted now.

'Why now?' Hayes muttered to himself as the other miners kept on firing their deadly weapons at their unseen attackers in the dense undergrowth.

'What changed to give them the vinegar to fight back?'

'If'n ya gonna think of something to git us out of this mess, Will,' Brown yelled over the noise of their gunfire, 'I sure wish ya'd do it fast.'

'We ain't got enough ammunition to last more than another hour or so,' Henson screamed down at their stunned leader. 'Ya got any tricks up ya sleeve?'

Tobey dropped down beside the shocked older man and slapped him hard across the face. 'Wake up, Will. Get ya rifle and start shooting before them critters get lucky again.'

Hayes' head rocked as a second blow caught him hard. He blinked, then angrily looked at Tobey. His left hand prevented the third slap from reaching its target.

'Who the hell do ya think ya hitting, Bob?' he snarled.

Tobey smiled. 'Welcome back. Now help us. Ya got a million tricks in that head of yours and we sure need one right now or we'll all end up skewcred like Rance. For pity's sake think of something, Will.'

Hayes swung around on his knees and stared round the edge of the crude entrance at the arrows which continued to fly at them. Then he cast his attention on the body of Bean lying in a pool of his own gore. He gritted his teeth and clenched his fists as his mind at last began to work.

'Git some matches,' Hayes ordered.

Tobey pushed himself up against the shoulder of the older man. 'Matches?'

'Yeah, matches.' Will Hayes slowly nodded as his eyes focused on the large mound of kindling. He raised his hand and pointed at it. 'I want that fire lit up.'

'Why?' Tobey asked anxiously as he withdrew a box of matches from his vest pocket and handed them to Hayes. 'If that fire's lit up it'll make us even easier to see. Their arrows ain't bin too far from the mark already. If that fire's raging we'll be sitting ducks.'

Hayes gave a slight shake of his head. 'Ya don't understand, Bob. That fire will save our bacon.'

'How?' Tobey questioned as his fellow miners kept on vainly firing their rifles at their hidden attackers. Attackers who were moving through the undergrowth after unloosening each arrow.

Hayes turned his head and looked at the troubled Tobey. 'Get the rest of the black powder together, Bob. I'll show ya how we make them critters quit. They're all gutless. It's gotta be that chief of theirs who has stirred them up against us. He must have told them that we ain't gods. We gotta prove him wrong. I have to bring the rest of his people back to their knees.'

'Their knees?' Tobey repeated the words.

Will Hayes got back to his feet as Rowe rolled the remaining barrel of black powder towards him from the back of the large hut where the rest of their belongings were stacked. Hayes glanced at Tobey and nodded.

'Yep. Their knees. How else they gonna pray to us, Bob?'

A cloudless night sky loomed across the vast empty range above the two riders as they forged on towards the forested mountains, which came closer with every stride of the two horses. The trail had been long and rugged for the two horsemen as they guided their mounts across the barren terrain towards the distant peaks. Hawkins hung close to the silent Iron Eyes as the emaciated rider allowed his powerful palomino to find its own pace. Whether the bounty hunter was steering the stallion his fellow rider could not tell. There appeared to be no movement in the man clad in undertaker's clothing.

The sheriff had been on many a long ride during his career as a starpacker but never before had he allowed a blind man to lead the way. Hawkins closed the distance between his horse and the big palomino until they were riding side by side. He kept looking at the moonlit face of his companion. A face which bore little resemblance to that of any other man he had ever set eyes upon during his long life.

'Ya sure they went this way, son?' the sheriff eventually asked. 'I ain't seen no hoof tracks at all.'

'The storm washed them away,' Iron Eyes muttered.

'But are ya sure this is the right trail?' Hawkins persisted.

'Yep. I'm dead sure, old-timer,' the bounty hunter said without turning his head. 'Trust me.'

Hawkins looked all around them. The eerie bluish light of the moon and a myriad stars gave the range an unholy feel about it to the nervous lawman. Hawkins raised the collar of his coat and shivered.

'They could have gone anywhere,' he pointed out. 'Maybe they rode east towards Waco?'

'Nope! They didn't head for Waco. They went the way we're headed, old-timer,' Iron Eyes said in a low, calm drawl. 'Have a little faith in me. I'll take ya right to their stinking hides.'

The lawman gave out a chuckle. 'Ya certain about that? Not a single doubt in that cement-cased skull of yours?'

'Nope. Not one little doubt at all.' Iron Eyes rubbed his eyes and looked straight ahead. He could see images illuminated by the bright moon. Images which were slowly becoming clearer as the night progressed.

'I must be loco tagging along with you,' Hawkins said with a shrug.

'I figured that out back at San Remo,' the bounty hunter replied. 'Only a locobean would want to ride with me.'

123

Hawkins rubbed his belly. 'Ain't we gonna stop and make camp for the night? I'm hungry and cold.'

'Ain't no time,' Iron Eyes muttered. 'Take a swig of some of my whiskey.'

'I might just do that, ya know?'

Without warning Iron Eyes eased back on his reins and stopped his stallion. The older rider did the same.

'Why ya stop?' Hawkins asked. He pulled a bottle of the fiery liquor from his saddlebag and pulled its cork. 'Change ya mind about making camp?'

The long left arm of the bounty hunter lifted up from the saddle horn it had been gripping. A thin finger pointed out into the darkness ahead of them.

'There,' Iron Eyes said.

After taking a mouthful of whiskey, Hawkins lifted himself up until he was balancing in his stirrups. He strained to see what the thin man was aiming his finger at.

'I don't see nothing,' he admitted. He replaced the cork into the neck of the bottle. 'Nothing at all.'

'Neither do I,' Iron Eyes said. His head turned slowly to face the sheriff. 'It ain't my eyes I'm heeding, old-timer. It's my nose and ears.'

'What?' Hawkins sat down again, replaced the bottle into his saddle-bag satchel and gathered up his loose reins in his gloved hands. He looked at the gruesome face of the horseman. 'Ya telling me that ya can smell and hear them?'

'Not them,' the bounty hunter corrected quietly. 'Their carcasses and the animals that are feeding off them, Sheriff.'

The head of the lawman jolted back to where the bony finger had been pointing. He tried to hear and failed. He then sniffed the air but still could not detect whatever it was Iron Eyes had been indicating.

'Ya reckon they're dead? Slater and Barker are lying dead out there?'

Iron Eyes lowered his arm and placed his hand back on top of the horn of his saddle. He tapped his spurs again. 'Something's sure dead out there. It's either them or some other poor critters who ran out of luck a few hours back.'

Hawkins urged his horse on and followed the stallion as it walked cautiously ahead. 'How could they be dead?'

'Beats the hell out of me, Sheriff,' the bounty hunter replied. 'But one thing I know for sure is that something's dead up yonder. Bet ya silver dollar it's them.'

'I might be loco but I'm not gonna bet against ya, Iron Eyes,' the sheriff said.

'Good.' The bounty hunter increased his pace by stabbing his spurs a few times. The lawman slapped the ends of his long reins across the shoulders of his saddle horse and caught up to the now galloping palomino.

'Hey. Are ya sure ya can't see, boy?' Hawkins

shouted out across the distance between the two thundering animals.

Iron Eyes did not reply.

FIFTEEN

The explosions came quick and fast after Hayes had ignited the massive bonfire into life with a well-aimed flaming torch. The natives had no answer to the black powder missiles thrown into the flames by the miners. Hayes had used his own well-worn shirt to make a handful of packages filled with the deadly explosive powder. His men had expertly cast them into the leaping flames to create the diversion the master magician had designed.

The exploding balls of black powder had shaken the camp and filled the entire area with choking smoke.

That was all the five men had required to free themselves from the large wigwam and rush out unseen by the Indians. Within a few heart-stopping seconds the heavily armed miners had managed to locate and kill a half-dozen of the stunned bowmen.

Unable to contain his emotions Hakatan had

bravely rushed out from his hiding-place with a tomahawk in his hand. He had charged at a speed which belied his age towards the smug-featured Hayes who held on to his smoking rifle in readiness to kill once more. But the vengeful wailing of the old Indian had betrayed him and alerted Hayes. Hakatan had not managed to reach his chosen target before all five of the prospectors had turned their rifles and fired at once. The bullets cut into the racing Indian and lifted his frail body off the ground. He tumbled over and over again across the wet ground, then slid helplessly into the river.

As soon as the tribal elder had disappeared into the foaming white water the entire area fell into silence. It was as if the tribe's heart had stopped beating.

The remaining Indians were herded up like animals and brought toward the flames. Only a few men remained alive, and even they were wounded. The majority of the surviving natives were female. Many were old. A handful were of an age which the miners had already mercilessly exploited. The rest were terrified children.

Hayes felt a sense of power overwhelming him. It was like nothing he had ever experienced before. Now he did not need any more magical trickery. He led the last of the village's braves to the water's edge and then lined them up with their backs to his smoking Winchester.

'This'll teach them, boys.' Hayes yelled out as he cocked the weapon his his hands. 'This'll teach them it no pay to mess with the gods.'

Still laughing Hayes fired at each of them in turn and watched as they all fell into the river. The light of the large bonfire illuminated their limp bodies as they were swept away in the swift current of the river.

Will Hayes turned to face the last of the cowering Indians and his men.

'Do what ya will with them, boys,' he yelled out triumphantly to the others as a sickening smile filled his features. 'Now we ain't got nothing to fear. Nothing at all.'

The miners did not require telling more than once. They moved like the two-legged vermin they were and dragged females up from the ground where they had been forced to kneel. The various ages of their victims meant nothing to them. The women would do what they were forced to do or face the consequences. Hayes laughed as he watched his men dragging them towards the largest of the huts.

What little clothing the females wore was torn from them even before they reached the entrance of the large gold-filled wigwam. Most of the females had already been whipped into submission long before this futile revolt. Their bodies bore the scars of previous abuse.

Then one of the youngest of the girls who had not been chosen jumped to her feet and raced across the open ground at the man who had orchestrated the destruction of her tribe. She was screaming as she tried to seek revenge for her loved ones.

It did not matter to Hayes that she was barely half his height. It did not matter that she was probably no more than eight years of age.

Will Hayes turned his rifle on her and then fired. The bullet lifted her off her feet. She crashed into the ground like a little rag doll,

He grabbed hold of her ankle, hauled her off the muddy soil and then tossed her into the raging torrent.

As he marched back to where his men had already started to service their victims he grabbed a child little bigger or older than the one he had just shot and thrown into the river. He dragged her screaming into the entrance of the hut.

The females and children who remained on their knees bathed in the light of the massive fire began to wail as one.

It was like a crescendo of ghosts.

SIXTEEN

The sun began to break across the vast range. Its light spread like wildfire until everything around the two men seemed to be ablaze. The sheriff had dismounted as soon as they reached the river whilst Iron Eyes sat astride his powerful stallion and struck a match across his saddle horn. The bounty hunter cupped its flame in his hands, touched the tip of his cigar and inhaled the strong acrid smoke deeply.

'Well?' Iron Eyes asked through a cloud of smoke. 'Is it them?'

Hawkins had dragged both bodies out of the water and turned them over. He compared the images on the wanted posters to the faces of the outlaws and then straightened up.

'Yep. It's them OK.' Sheriff Hawkins returned the posters to the outheld left hand of the thin horseman as he again looked down on the corpses of the dead outlaws which were stranded on the bank of the river. Both bodies showed proof that they had been mauled by wild animals since they had arrived at the crook in the river. 'How'd ya manage to find them without being able to see, Iron Eyes?'

'Can't ya smell them, Sheriff?'

'Nope,' Hawkins admitted.

'How'd they die?' Iron Eyes asked.

The light of the morning sun showed the lawman the multiple bullet holes in both outlaws' torsos. The blood had been washed away but not the evidence of the burnt shirt fronts. A black mark surrounded each of the bullet holes. Hawkins rubbed his neck and exhaled loudly. 'They're riddled with bullets, boy. Whoever shot them sure made sure they was dead. I never seen such a lot of holes in two men's chests.'

'I hate folks who waste lead,' Iron Eyes sighed. 'One or two bullets ought to be enough to kill anyone. Why waste so much? It just don't make no sense.'

'I don't get it either.' Hawkins held on to his reins and looked across the river up into the forested valley ahead of them. It seemed an eerie place even bathed in sunlight.

'What don't ya get?'

The sheriff bit his lower lip thoughtfully. 'Why did the critters who killed 'em just leave them here and not take them down into San Remo to collect the reward money? Why leave 'em here?'

'They didn't kill them here, Joe,' Iron Eyes said bluntly.

'What?' Sheriff Hawkins looked up at the fearsome figure who still sucked on the black cigar. 'What ya mean, they weren't killed here? If not here, where was they killed?'

'They were just washed down here from somewhere upriver,' the bounty hunter asserted confidently. 'I figure that whoever killed them didn't know they were wanted. Either that or they didn't care or need the reward.'

Hawkins stepped closer to the horseman with smoke trailing from his lips. 'How'd ya know they was killed upriver?'

'See their horses anywhere?' Iron Eyes asked, waving his free hand around expressively.

'They could have run off or bin stolen by the killers,' the lawman argued.

'Maybe,' the thin man said. 'I just don't think so.'

The sheriff gave the valley another long look. 'Upriver means right in the heart of that forest. Damned if I'd wanna head on up into that place if there was another trail I could take. Nobody ever goes thataway.'

'I would.'

'But you ain't normal, boy,' Hawkins said.

Iron Eyes felt his eyes burning again. He blinked and looked down at the figure standing beside the neck of his mount. 'Damn it all. I can see again.'

133

Hawkins's expression changed. 'Ya can? Can ya see clearly?'

'Yep,' the bounty hunter answered before adding; 'Hell, I forgot just how ugly ya was, old-timer.'

Hawkins shook his head. 'Enough joking, handsome. We gonna put these bodies on the backs of our nags and take them back to town?'

'I don't reckon so,' Iron Eyes replied as he lifted himself off his saddle and squinted out across the river to the other bank.

'Why not?'

'That.' Iron Eyes pulled the cigar from his teeth and pointed with it at something across the river. Something which made him sit back down, tap his spurs against the flanks of his stallion and head into the fast-moving river. 'C'mon!'

'What ya seen, boy?' Hawkins grabbed his saddle horn and stepped into his stirrup. He hauled himself on top of his horse and urged it to follow the bounty hunter. Spray plumed up to either side of him as the lawman tried to catch up with the strange bounty hunter.

Iron Eyes remained silent until his horse reached the opposite bank of the river. He allowed the stallion to walk up on to the dry ground and then slowly dismounted. He held on to his reins and stared down into the reeds. His expression suddenly altered. All humour was drained from him.

'Hell! That ain't the sort of thing I wanted to see

when my eyes healed up,' Iron Eyes drawled to himself.

'What ya found?' Hawkins asked when his saddle horse had scrambled up on to the riverbank next to the palomino. The puzzled lawman dismounted. 'Well? What is it?'

'Something bad. Real bad.' Iron Eyes handed his reins to the sheriff, then stepped into the water and stooped down. He lifted a small girl out of the river and turned to face his companion.

'Hell. That's a little girl,' the sheriff gasped. 'A little Indian girl by the looks of it.'

Cradling the child Iron Eyes walked away from the water until he came to a dry patch of grass. He bent down, placed the chilled girl on to the grass and knelt down beside her. He removed his long coat, placed it over her, then rested a finger against her neck.

'Is she alive, Iron Eyes?'

The bounty hunter rose up to his full height. He removed the cigar from his lips and then threw it away angrily.

'Nope.'

The visibly upset lawman bent over the small body and peeled the coat back. His eyes spotted the bullet hole and he turned his head to tell Iron Eyes. But the bounty hunter had already thrown himself on to the back of the palomino.

'She was shot, boy,' Hawkins said.

'I know.' Iron Eyes snarled, spurred his horse and thundered up into the valley. 'Ya coming?'

Hawkins replaced the coat over the little girl and hastily mounted. He slapped his reins across the rear of his horse and raced after the bounty hunter along the river's edge.

'Where ya going, boy?' the sheriff called out as he drew level with Iron Eyes.

Gripping his reins in both hands, Iron Eyes glanced at the sheriff and yelled out, 'I'm going to kill me the dirty varmints who done that to that little un, old-timer. OK?'

'OK!' Hawkins called back.

SEVENTEEN

It had been an unrelenting ride which had taken them until long after the sun had set once more. They had passed a dozen or more totem poles before darkness had overwhelmed the valley, and as many again beneath the light of the bright moon. The coming of night had not slowed their determined pace. They had forged on along the muddy trail beside the edge of the river in resolute pursuit of the killer of the small child.

For hours the sheriff and the bounty hunter had followed the tracks left by the outlaws' horses, until Iron Eyes spotted something and drew rein. There was a strange eerie light which pervaded the forest, yet it was enough for the seasoned hunter to see what he had been looking for. The large palomino stallion stopped, then lowered its head. It was lathered up and exhausted but, like its determined master, it stubbornly refused to quit.

'Hold these.' Iron Eyes threw his reins to Hawkins, swung his leg over the palomino's neck and slid to the ground. His light frame made no sound as he landed in the soft mud.

'What ya seen there, boy?' the sheriff asked. He steadied his own horse whilst holding on to his companion's reins.

The thin figure dropped to one knee and placed the palm of his hand on the wet mud. He then studied the surrounding area until he got the whole picture of the events that had occurred at this very spot.

'Answer me, Iron Eyes. What's them tracks telling ya?' Hawkins begged the kneeling man for answers.

The bounty hunter stood up and looked all around him. There was a hint of confusion in his twisted features. Then he closed his eyes and listened to the valley and forest as if it were speaking to him. He rested a hand on the withers of his stallion and looked up at the sheriff.

'This is where Slater and Barker were killed.' Iron Eyes said with assurance. 'This is where they died and were rolled into the river. I'm certain of that much, but there's something else that don't figure. It don't figure at all.'

'How many of them were there that done for them outlaws?'

'Five to start with and then a sixth.' Iron Eyes said confidently.

'Then what's got ya so confused?' Hawkins leaned over from his high perch. 'I never seen ya look so bewildered.'

Iron Eyes looked upward at the low-hanging mist. 'All the signs say that the sixth *hombre* flew in like a bird.'

Hawkins straightened up. He expression said more than any words which might leave his lips would dare to. 'Come again?'

Iron Eyes pointed up at the sky. 'The last man to set about killing them outlaws flew in from over yonder. At first I thought he must have bin up in a tree and just dropped down on them but that ain't how it happened. He flew in.'

'Flew in?'

'Yep.' The bounty hunter led his horse to the edge of the river where tall clusters of reeds rose from the water. He allowed the stallion to drink as his brain fought to understand the clues which surrounded them. Clues which seemed incredible even to him. After a few minutes of silence, Iron Eyes looked at the sheriff and continued his theorizing. 'By my reckoning, he flew across the river. From over there to right about here and then he dropped out of the sky.'

Hawkins eyebrows rose. 'Is that skull of yours playing ya up again, boy?'

'Nope.' Iron Eyes opened one of the satchels of his saddle-bags and drew out a bottle. He pulled its

139

cork and then took a long welcome swallow of the whiskey. He offered the bottle to Hawkins who accepted. The sheriff downed a mouthful, then handed the bottle back to his companion. 'I ain't loco, Joe. I'm telling you what the signs say happened.'

'A man can't fly, son.'

A wry grin crossed the face of Iron Eyes. 'He can if he's rigged up some wires.'

'What?'

The bony fingers of the bounty hunter pointed at the moonlit sky. 'Open them eyes of yours, old-timer. Look hard and you'll see them. Wires.'

Hawkins looked up and was about to say something when he caught sight of the wire, which was right above them. The light of the moon danced along its entire length. 'Damn it all. There's a couple of wires up there. Who'd wanna rig up something like that and why? It don't make sense.'

'There's another one going over there.' Iron Eyes pointed a finger and watched as the sheriff nodded in bemused agreement. 'See it?'

'Yeah,' Hawkins said. 'What I don't see is a reason for a man to fly, boy.'

Iron Eyes squinted hard at the ground and then scooped up a small bright object. He handed it to his friend. 'Is this what I think it is, Joe?'

Hawkins rubbed the mud from the gold nugget and gasped. 'It sure is. Gold.'

Iron Eyes thought about the body of the little girl they had discovered earlier that day. The body that he had left wrapped in his long frock-coat. 'Listen up. We know there must be Injuns in this forest, Sheriff. That little gal is proof of that. We also know that there must be mighty ruthless white folks in here as well. Now we know that there's gold here. It all fits. I figure we're hunting a bunch of prospectors. Gold prospectors.'

'And Injuns in this forest might not like folks panning for their gold,' Hawkins said thoughtfully.

'Maybe the wires and a man flying is meant to hoodwink them.'

'Yeah,' Hawkins agreed. 'But whatever the truth is, all I can think about is that poor little gal we found back there and the stinking bastard who killed her.'

'Not only killed her but threw her body into the river like she was trash,' Iron Eyes growled like a mountain cat. 'Yeah. Just like they done with Barker and Slater. I can understand someone doing that to outlaws but not a helpless kid.'

'We'll make 'em pay, boy.' Hawkins nodded his determination.

'Pay with their worthless hides,' Iron Eyes added. he took another swig from his bottle, then pushed it back into his saddle-bag.

The sheriff stared at the gruesome-looking bounty hunter. He had never seen the man so visibly upset or angry before. Even when faced with the fearsome

Kansas Drew McGinty Iron Eyes had remained totally detached. There had been no hint either of fear or remorse when he had so expertly killed the outlaw.

Now Iron Eyes was engulfed by fury. A fury which equalled his own resolve. But was the pitifully ill-looking man fit enough to make his words reality? The question troubled the lawman.

'How's them eyes of yours?' the sheriff asked. 'They still holding up? Can ya still see good?'

'Good enough,' came the low, growling response. 'I don't need eyes to kill me vermin though, Sheriff. Ya already know I only needs my guns for that.'

'As long as ya feels up to carrying on.'

Again Iron Eyes studied the ground around them, then he looked towards the river. He moved around both horses like a panther stalking its prey, his eyes burning at the signs on the muddy surface leading to the water. Then he raised a hand to alert the lawman of something he had noticed. Hawkins gripped his holstered gun and watched as Iron Eyes waded out into the river until its water lapped over the top of his high boots.

Even in the water the hunter did not make any sound. He moved silently in a half-circle around the bed of reeds until he saw the thing his senses had alerted him to. He signalled with his left hand at the sheriff. Hawkins dismounted.

'Come here, Joe,' Iron Eyes said firmly as he waded into a thicket of tall reeds and stooped out of

142

sight. Hawkins rushed out into the river until he was next to his companion. Then to his surprise he saw the thin man hauling something out of the reed bed. He helped Iron Eyes steady himself against the current and followed him back to the riverbank.

'Is that another body?' Hawkins asked as his eyes tried to see what the younger man had discovered.

'Another Injun.' Iron Eyes said through gritted teeth. He carried Hakatan's cold body back to the shore.

Joe Hawkins watched as Iron Eyes placed the limp Indian tribal elder on the ground and knelt down beside him.

'Is he dead like the others, boy?'

Iron Eyes looked up. 'Nope. He ain't dead at all. He's got himself a couple of rifle bullets in him but his heart is beating real powerful.'

'He might still be alive now, but he ain't gonna last long if we don't get him warmed up.' Hawkins hurried to his horse and dragged his bedroll from behind the saddle cantle. He unfolded it, tossed it over Hakatan, then knelt down next to the bounty hunter. 'We need us a fire.'

Iron Eyes did not respond. He just kept rubbing the man's hands feverishly in an attempt to get the Indian's blood flowing round him again.

'Another rifle-shot victim,' the sheriff muttered. 'Somebody up yonder must be having themselves a real good time shooting folks.'

'Yeah,' the bounty hunter agreed. 'Even loco prospectors don't kill this many folks unless they're protecting something. Something real valuable.'

'Like a fortune in gold nuggets.'

Iron Eyes narrowed his eyes and stared up river to where the trees concealed a bend in its course.

'I reckon they must have themselves a camp just round that turn in the river. Leastways, that's what the signs all say.'

Hawkins watched the younger man as he wrapped the blanket even more tightly around the wounded brave. Then he touched the arm of the bounty hunter. 'Are ya really OK, son?'

'Light a fire to warm this old fella up,' Iron Eyes said.

The sheriff nodded. 'We leaving him here?'

The bounty hunter gave a slow nod. 'Yep. We'll come back for him if things go our way.'

'What ya thinking, son?' Hawkins asked. 'I got me a feeling in my craw it ain't got nothing to do with no campfire.'

'Ya right. I'm thinking about that little girl, old-timer,' Iron Eyes answered.

'Is that all?'

'Nope.' Iron Eyes stood and checked his Navy Colts in turn before pushing them back into his pants belt. 'I'm also thinking about killing me the bastards who killed her.'

'Me too.'

The vicious attack had gone on for more than twenty-four hours within the Indian camp and seemed set to continue until the prospectors either ran out of stamina or lost their appetite for doing their worst. Few of the surviving natives had been spared the brutal whippings Will Hayes and his men dished out for any disobedience. The huge fire in the very centre of the clearing had been constantly replenished by the women and children throughout the endless hours of merciless savagery. Yet in spite of the heat of the raging bonfire, there was a cold chill in the air of the ancient settlement.

Hayes and his four fellow goldminers were drunk. Not with the effects of alcohol but with unchallenged power. It seemed that whatever the age of the natives they were not immune to the brutal whippings of their self-appointed masters. Blood and scars both old and fresh covered all of the natives' near-naked bodies. It was painful not to obey and do their masters' bidding.

No medieval tyrants could have abused their power over the weaker and more peaceful souls with more severity. No longer hindered by the necessity to masquerade as gods and to kill the tribe's menfolk, the prospectors were wallowing in their own filth.

The miners were truly intoxicated. Their inhumanity seemed to reach down to new depths with every passing heartbeat. It was now a certainty that few if any of the forest's original children would survive to witness the departure of Hayes and the others when they finally left with their spoils.

Iron Eyes and Sheriff Hawkins reined back as their horses reached the bend in the river. Unlike the outlaws their approach had gone unnoticed by the men who wrongly thought that they no longer had any enemies to worry about. The bushes here, close to the bend of the wood-fringed river's edge were sparce. Both horsemen had an unobstructed view of the horrors which were happening ahead of them in the Indian camp. The blazing bonfire illuminated the heart of the small settlement as brightly as day, even though it was close to midnight.

For what felt like a lifetime the horsemen watched with a growing sense of anger and revulsion. It was Iron Eyes who looked away first. He felt sick.

A mere few seconds later Hawkins lowered his eyes and gave a long sigh. 'Damn it all, boy. I'd thought I'd seen most things but I ain't never witnessed nothing like that.'

Iron Eyes did not speak. He drew long, slow breaths and tried to swallow as the pitiful screams of women and children washed over him. Then his long left arm reached back and groped for a whiskey bottle.

The lawman looked at him. 'Can I have me a gutful of that stuff when ya through, son?'

The bounty hunter swallowed a good quarter-pint, then handed the bottle to the sheriff. He still did not utter a word as he tried to calm himself down.

Hawkins almost matched the volume of fiery liquor he poured down his own throat, then he returned the bottle to the silent man astride the high-shouldered palomino. 'Thanks.'

Iron Eyes replaced the cork and pushed the bottle back down into the leather satchel behind his high Mexican saddle cantle. He gathered up his reins and gritted his teeth as he looked all about the area. The river was fast-moving, but held no fear for the bounty hunter.

'What's ya aiming to do?' the sheriff asked.

'I'm heading across the river,' Iron Eyes replied.

'Why?' Hawkins's eyebrows rose towards his hat brim. 'Them varmints are less than two hundred yards ahead of us. We could ride on in there and kill them with their pants down. Why cross over the river?'

'I got me a plan, old-timer.' Iron Eyes produced a two-foot square sheet of oilskin from his saddle-bags and wrapped his guns in it. 'I want you to stay here.'

The lawman scratched his chin as Iron Eyes pushed the guns inside his shirt. 'I don't get it.'

'You will.'

Sheriff Hawkins leaned closer and looked hard at the gaunt horseman. 'What ya figuring on doing, Iron Eyes? What's going on in that busted head of yours?'

Iron Eyes remained silent. He removed his coiled rope from his saddle, shook it loose, then looped its end around a sturdy boulder. He tightened it whilst firmly tying the other end round the silver saddle horn. A broad grin spread across the cruelly scarred features of the bounty hunter.

'What ya up to, boy?' the lawman asked.

A bony hand patted the wide-eyed sheriff's cheek.

'Use this rope to haul my horse back to this side when I signal ya.' Iron Eyes instructed.

'Why ya heading over there for?' Hawkins asked again.

'I'm gonna fly, Joe.'

'Ya could break ya neck,' the older man said. 'Don't be stupid. It's suicide.'

'I ain't the one that's gonna die, old-timer.'

Before the lawman could object the bounty hunter hauled his reins hard to his right, stabbed his spurs into the palomino and rode into the fast-flowing river. Within seconds the horse was up to its neck and fighting the current. Hawkins watched helplessly as the mighty stallion swam toward the opposite bank with its intrepid master clinging to the saddle horn.

'Damn it all,' Hawkins cursed. 'I hope that rope is long enough.'

For more than two thirds of its width the river had proved a fierce challenge even for the mighty palomino stallion. The last fifty or so feet had been shallow enough for the horse to find its feet and carry its bedraggled master to the opposite bank. Iron Eyes fell from the high back of the exhausted animal as though every ounce of his strength had been drained from his thin body. For more than five minutes the bounty hunter lay where he had fallen, holding on to his reins and staring up into the branches of the tree he knew he would have to climb.

Eventually he managed to summon all his energies into getting back on to his feet again. He stared out to where he had left his companion. Hawkins still sat astride his saddle horse watching Iron Eyes' every move, awaiting the signal. Iron Eyes rested against the saddle of the stallion. He felt a strange pain inside his head and he raised both hands to check that the cement cast was still in place. To his surprise, it was.

Again he looked up into the dark shadows above him. The wire had been rigged by an expert and was strong enough to take his pitiful weight, he concluded.

Iron Eyes pulled the guns from inside his shirt and carefully unfolded the oilskin. They were dry and ready for action. He pushed their cold barrels into his pants belt, then ripped his soaked shirt from his scarred torso. He cast the shirt aside and untied the saddle-bags from behind the cantle. Iron Eyes checked inside both satchels. A bottle of his precious whiskey rested in each of them. He placed the saddle-bags over his shoulders so that one satchel hung to each side. He checked that his long thin arms could reach the necks of the bottles. He nodded to himself.

'That oughta do it,' Iron Eyes drawled. He turned the horse round until it faced his partner across the fast-flowing river. Silently the bounty hunter signalled to Hawkins. He watched as the older man started to haul on the long rope. Reluctantly the stallion walked into the river and began the taxing journey back to the opposite riverbank.

With the agility of a mountain cat, Iron Eyes climbed up the trunk of the tree until he reached a high branch more than thirty feet above the ground.

His icy stare was drawn back to the scene around the blazing campfire. The sickening screams filled his ears again and fuelled his already raging fury.

Balancing on a sturdy branch Iron Eyes unbuckled his belt from his pants and cast it over the wire above him. He refastened its buckle. He placed an arm and his head through the looped leather and checked that it could take his weight.

His eyes narrowed. All he could see were the prospectors doing their worst around the huge fire as its flames leapt up into the night sky.

Without an ounce of fear Iron Eyes sprang away from the tree with only his two-inch-wide belt between himself and a long deadly fall. Within seconds he was hurtling over the raging river, down along the wire, at a speed he had never imagined possible towards the small Indian village. Smoke and then flames began to trail from the leather belt as the friction grew more and more intense the faster Iron Eyes travelled along the wire.

Holding on for dear life the ghostly figure cleared the wide river and headed on towards the heart of the clearing. Then Iron Eyes crossed directly over the campfire. He hauled his precious bottles of whiskey from the saddle-bags and hurled them both down into the middle of the flames. The bottles shattered, expelling their spirituous contents in all directions.

Suddenly the flames were alive. A fiery fountain rose upward behind the hurtling bounty hunter. He felt its heat burning his back. Blazing rain showered over the large wigwam, catching its dry fabric alight. A ball of fire rose a hundred feet into the night sky.

Yet before Will Hayes or any of his evil followers had time to realize what was happening, the belt holding their attacker aloft burned through and broke.

Iron Eyes felt himself falling towards the ground at incredible speed. Like a cat he turned before his lean frame hit the floor of the valley. His bony hands drew both guns, cocked their hammers and fired at two of the miners a split second before he crashed into the unforgiving soil.

Winded, the bounty hunter lay motionless for what felt like an eternity. Then through the smoke

151

that his burning whiskey had created Iron Eyes saw both Pete Brown and Clint Henson knocked off their feet by his well-placed bullets. Neither would ever rise again.

The native women and children scattered into the undergrowth as Hayes mustered Sly Rowe and Bob Tobey to arms. The three men grabbed their rifles and began their search amid the choking smoke.

The bounty hunter felt as if he had just been run over by a herd of buffalo, yet he managed to force himself off the hard ground with his smoking weapons still clutched in his hands.

Blood ran freely from both his nostrils as his narrowed eyes focused on the last three of the miners as they came charging away from the large burning hut. Tobey and Rowe spotted him first. Rods of white-hot lead vainly chased the winded figure across the clearing as Iron Eyes somehow managed to run for cover.

Bullets tore all around the shaken Iron Eyes as his long legs somehow carried him behind one of the smaller huts. He cocked his gun hammers again and tried to steady himself against the thin wall of the Indian dwelling.

Then another deafening volley of bullets cut through the hut's thin walls, all around his slender frame. He felt the burning in his leg and instinctively knew he had been winged but refused to acknowledge the pain that ripped through him. Iron Eyes turned and jumped down on to the ground. He rolled over and over as Rowe and Tobey came running out of the black smoke.

There was no hint of alarm at the sight of the two men charging towards him. The fearless bounty hunter squeezed both triggers in turn. Rowe was knocked off his feet as one of the well-aimed bullets went into his temple and shattered his skull. Tobey was hit low in the guts and staggered on until a second shot found his chest. As the second of his targets landed heavily beside him, Iron Eyes got to his knees and searched the area for the last of the heartless men he sought.

Then he saw him.

Realizing that he was alone, Will Hayes backed off towards the large building, which was now well ablaze. As the flames swept over the ancient wigwam he was almost tempted to rush in after the fortune in gold that was still harboured within its burning walls.

Then Hayes saw the gruesome Iron Eyes rising to his full height beside the bodies of Rowe and Tobey. The smoking barrels of the Navy Colts hung in Iron Eyes' bony hands at his sides.

With smoke billowing between them, Hayes frantically cranked the mechanism of his Winchester and swiftly fired at the approaching bounty hunter.

Shot after shot left the long barrel of the repeating rifle as the magician tried to kill the unholy-looking creature who doggedly moved silently towards him. Hayes could not believe that none of his bullets had found their target. Yet if they had how was this monster with a cement skullcap and long, limp hair still walking?

Hayes had seen most things in his life. The carnival freak show was not new to him but nothing had prepared his burning eyes for what he saw looming at him through the twisting acrid smoke of the raging inferno.

'What are ya?' Hayes screamed out as his trigger finger fired the last of his bullets at the man, who yet walked through the flames straight at him. 'What are ya?'

Iron Eyes stopped, cocked both gun hammers and raised his arms in one fluid movement. He did not answer the question but asked one of his own.

'Was it you who killed that little gal and threw her in the river?' the bounty hunter yelled back over the noise of the unchecked fire.

'What?' Hayes turned the rifle upside down and gripped its hot barrel. He was prepared to use it as a club should the strange apparition get any closer. 'Ya talking about that little stinking Injun kid? Sure it was me. What's it got to do with the likes of you, anyway?'

Iron Eyes squeezed both triggers. His deadly accuracy did not fail him. Both his bullets hit Hayes between the eyes. There was not a whisker between them. The head of the defiant man was destroyed by the powerful impact. Hayes fell lifeless into the flames.

With the sound of the shots still echoing around the clearing, Hawkins ran cautiously through the smoke with his gun drawn, to the side of the towering bounty hunter. His eyes darted around the area.

'Any of them left, boy?'

'Don't fret none, Joe. They're all dead. They ain't gonna kill no more little 'uns.' Iron Eyes pushed the smoking barrels into his pants and walked away.

FINALE

Iron Eyes was patting the earth down with his bare hands as the sheriff rode up to him and leaned on his saddle horn. Hawkins bit his lower lip and watched the bounty hunter as the thin man pulled on his black frock-coat again.

'That old Injun we found in the river is still alive, boy,' Hawkins said. 'I took him back to their camp. Them women and kids were there. They was sure badly beaten up.'

Iron Eyes did not speak. He rubbed the mud from his hands down the front of his coat, then turned to where his horse was tethered. He limped towards it.

'That leg playing ya up?' the lawman enquired.

The bounty hunter pulled his reins free and looked at Hawkins. There seemed to be no expression in his gaunt face, except pain. Only pain.

'Don't ya ever stop gabbing, old-timer?' he asked as he lifted his leg, poked the tip of his left boot into the stirrup and hauled his lean frame up and on to the tall stallion. 'Seems to me that anyone as old as you are would have run out of words to say by now.'

Hawkins edged his mount closer to the palomino and its solemn master. He pushed the brim of his hat back on his head until his white hair could be seen against his tanned face.

'Ya buried her deep, boy?' the older horseman asked. He glanced at the grave.

Iron Eyes nodded. 'Yep. Good and deep so the wild critters will leave her alone. They can smell death up to six feet down, ya know?'

'I know.' Hawkins gathered his reins and watched as the bounty hunter touched his still bleeding thigh. 'Ya need stitching up again, son.'

'Yep.' Iron Eyes turned the powerful horse until it was aimed back at the distant range. 'Reckon I'd better head on back to that town of yours. I need me some hard liquor real bad.'

'Good idea.' Hawkins urged his mount on. The palomino walked beside the smaller horse along the river's edge. 'We can pick up them outlaws' bodies on the way so ya can collect the bounty.'

'I didn't kill them varmints though.' Iron Eyes muttered.

'What does it matter?' Hawkins shrugged as both horses began to increase their pace. 'Ya killed the varmints who did and that's as good as killing them in my book, boy.'

'Reckon so.' Iron Eyes was holding his reins firmly. 'When I get me back to San Remo I'll buy me a whole lot of whiskey and a brand-new red shirt and a new pair of pants.'

'A red shirt?' Sheriff Hawkins smiled. 'Ain't that kinda bright for the likes of you?'

Iron Eyes tilted his head back. 'Red don't show the blood so easy, Joe.'

Hawkins chuckled. 'Least ya can see old Doc again when we gets to town.'

Iron Eyes turned his head.

'I sure hope so, old-timer.'

'What ya mean, boy?'

'I ain't seen nothing at all since I shot that bastard who killed the little gal.' Iron Eyes turned his head back to face the trail ahead of them.

'What?' Hawkins swallowed hard.

'I'm blind again, friend. Totally blind.'

The two horsemen continued on.